A Promise of Forever Love

A Promise of Forever Love

Vanessa Miller

WHITAKER
HOUSE

A PROMISE OF FOREVER LOVE
Book Three in the Second Chance at Love Series

Vanessa Miller
www.vanessamiller.com

ISBN: 978-1-60374-209-2
Printed in the United States of America
© 2011 by Vanessa Miller

Whitaker House
1030 Hunt Valley Circle
New Kensington, PA 15068
www.whitakerhouse.com

Library of Congress Cataloging-in-Publication Data

Miller, Vanessa.
  A promise of forever love / by Vanessa Miller.
      p. cm. — (Second chance at love ; bk. 3)
  ISBN 978-1-60374-209-2 (trade pbk.)
  1. Widows—Fiction. 2. Women clergy—Fiction. 3. African American churches—Fiction. I. Title.
  PS3613.I5623P86 2011
  813'.6—dc22

                                    2010051282

1 2 3 4 5 6 7 8 9 10 **WH** 17 16 15 14 13 12 11

Prologue

O N DAYS LIKE THIS, YVONNE MILNER WONDERED WHY SHE even bothered to pray. She had yelled, screamed, begged, and cajoled, yet the doctors avoided making eye contact with her when they came into her husband's hospital room. There were no more talks of surgery or chemotherapy. They'd told her that nothing more could be done for David. But, as far as Yvonne was concerned, the doctors didn't know diddly. David Milner was the senior pastor of one of the most notable churches in Detroit. He was the father of two beautiful daughters, and he was her beloved husband. So, she wasn't just going to throw in the towel and believe the doctors' doom-and-gloom predictions. She and David had been married for thirty-four years, and he had promised her a fiftieth wedding anniversary celebration. "We've got sixteen more years to go, David," she urged him. "Don't give up now."

A vicious cough shook his fragile, cancer-racked body as he attempted to sit up in his hospital bed.

"Don't, sweetheart. Just lie down."

"No...I need...to tell you...something." David labored to get each word out.

It was killing Yvonne to see her husband weak and bedridden like this. He had always been so strong, had always been her hero. She had admired this man, even when they hadn't seen eye-to-eye about her role in the ministry. Early in their marriage, Yvonne had known that she was destined to preach the gospel. However, David wouldn't hear of it. They had fought, and Yvonne had prayed for years that God would change her husband's mind. Finally, David had accepted the fact that his wife had been called by God to be a preacher. Yet, even through those tough years, Yvonne couldn't have imagined being anywhere but with the man she loved. "You can say what you need to while lying down, honey. You need your strength to get better."

David shook his head. "I'm going home, baby."

"I know that, David. You just need to regain your strength so they will let you out of this hospital."

He shook his head again and then pointed heavenward. "Home...with Jesus."

Yvonne's eyes filled with tears. "Don't say that, David. You and I have a lot more living to do."

He patted her hand. "Call Thomas."

Thomas Reed was David's best friend. The man traveled the world, building churches and ministering to God's people. He'd recently lost his wife to the same evil disease that was threatening to take David's life. "Call Thomas right now? Why? What do you want me to tell him?"

"If you need help, call Thomas. He promised me—" A coughing fit cut him off.

Yvonne took the cup from David's bedside table and filled it with water from the pitcher, then held it to his lips for him to drink once the coughing subsided. "Here, baby, drink this." When he had taken a few sips, she said, "Now, just lie here and rest. Our girls will be here soon, and you need to save your energy for them." Toya, twenty-six years old, was their firstborn, a self-assured attorney with political aspirations. Tia was their twenty-four-year-old "baby." While Toya was analytical and ambitious, Tia's strength was creativity, yet she was introspective and reserved. She could paint and write poetry from sunup till sundown and be perfectly at peace.

It had been difficult for Yvonne to manage her daughters' very different personalities while raising them, but David had convinced her to relax and let God work out His perfect plan for each girl's life. If it hadn't been for David's wisdom and prayers, Yvonne was sure that she would have broken Tia's spirit. She had needed more time than David to understand their daughter's passion for the creative arts. What was she going to do if he didn't survive this illness?

No sooner had the thought crossed her mind than Yvonne tried to banish it. But that was also the moment when she noticed that David's breathing sounded funny. And then she understood why none of the medical professionals who had come into the room today had been able to look her in the eye. They had heard it, too—the death rattle.

"No, baby, no—don't leave me!" she begged him.

"Remember...Thomas promised...love you."

Tears were running down Yvonne's face as she heard her husband's last words. She put her arms around the man she had loved for a lifetime—and yet not long enough—and whispered, "I love you, too, baby. Always and forever."

Chapter One

Eighteen months later

YVONNE MILNER COLLAPSED INTO HER OFFICE CHAIR and heaved a sigh. Pastoring Christ-Life Sanctuary by herself was far from easy, and it seemed that her situation was only getting worse. For years, the church had grown and thrived; it had even reached megachurch status with more than five thousand members. But since David's death, two thousand of their "You can count on me" members had left the ministry. The head elder, Ron Thompson, had broken away to start his own ministry, taking another two hundred church members with him. Tithing was down, charity fund expenditures were up, and Yvonne knew that the church's board of directors blamed it all on her.

Several of the board members had challenged her authority to her face and as good as said that they wouldn't be having those problems if David were still around or if their senior pastor wasn't a woman. Yvonne acknowledged that some people could not accept having a female in the highest position of church leadership, but she also knew that not all twenty-two hundred members had left for that reason.

Sighing again, she stood up and stepped over to the bay window to gaze out at the new Family Life Center— or, rather, what was supposed to be the new Family Life Center, the final phase of their latest building project. The Family Life Center had been her vision. After the sanctuary had been expanded to make room for their growing congregation, Yvonne had convinced David that they still needed to do more. She had envisioned a brand-new facility that would provide space for recreational activities, especially for the children and young adults, as well as a café and a bookstore. In addition, she had intended for one of the rooms to be set up theater-style, with tiered seats and a movie screen, where they could organize movie nights or perform stage plays.

Five years ago, when Yvonne and David had first proposed the building project to the board, they had developed a financial plan based on the church's finances and projected that they would have more than enough funds to cover each phase of the project. But Yvonne hadn't foreseen the death of her husband or the annihilation of Detroit's economy. How could she have known that General Motors and Chrysler would go crying to the government for a bailout and then lay off thousands upon thousands of workers, many of whom attended church at Christ-Life Sanctuary?

Now Yvonne was stuck staring at a half finished Family Life Center, as it would probably remain. After all, the coffers were empty. She really couldn't blame the board of directors for asking for her resignation. While her husband had been alive, Yvonne had stood side by side with him as they'd built this church from the ground up. She had installed three of their seven board members herself. And she knew that God wasn't finished with her yet. The work He had begun in her—and in the church through her ministry—was far from over, and she would be dead and buried before anyone took her out of the pulpit permanently. She just needed a plan, needed to pray about knowing the right things to say at the board meeting tomorrow in order to convince the members to give her more time to turn things around.

A knock at her door drew Yvonne's eyes away from the window. She turned toward the sound. "Come in."

The door opened, and in walked Thomas Reed. Actually, he didn't walk; he swaggered like a man who had the keys to the kingdom. If she hadn't known Thomas for almost thirty years, Yvonne would have thought he swaggered so confidently because he was a millionaire several times over. But Thomas had strutted like that even when he had been as poor as a man carrying a "Will work for food" sign.

Thomas had a way about him that caused men and women alike to stop and stare. He was one of those fine, chocolate, Denzel Washington types of brothers, with wavy black hair and heavenly hazel eyes.

David had met Thomas thirty years ago in seminary and had joked about marrying Yvonne to keep her away from pretty boys like Thomas so that he didn't have to worry about her running off. But David had never had reason to worry; he had always been her prince, and she'd never wanted anyone but him.

When Thomas got married, David became less worried about his friend's captivating charm. The four of them—David and Yvonne, Thomas and Brenda—had settled into their own ministries yet maintained a lasting friendship. David and Yvonne opened Christ-Life Sanctuary a year after David graduated from seminary, and the church had flourished from its inception. Thomas, on the other hand, was forced to close the doors to his church after struggling for five years to make a go of it. He hadn't let that stop him, though. Thomas became a Christ-centered motivational speaker and took his ministry on the road. He now pulled in fifty thousand dollars per speaking engagement. He also had written nearly a dozen *New York Times* best-selling books.

"Thomas!" Yvonne gave him a hug and stepped back to admire his suit. "Look at you, dapper as ever on this hot summer day."

"You don't look so bad, yourself," he said with a grin.

"I can't believe you came all this way."

"I wouldn't miss this board meeting for anything in the world. And besides, I have a promise to make good on."

Just before David died, he had told Yvonne to call Thomas if she ever needed help. She'd seen Thomas at the funeral, where he had asked if she needed anything. No, she'd said, and for eighteen months, she hadn't bothered her husband's best friend for assistance, even though he'd called her from time to time to check in. But today, she was finally calling in a favor. Thomas had been installed as a board member of Christ-Life Sanctuary about ten years ago but rarely showed up for meetings. The board had always been in accord with David, so he'd never needed to rely on his friend for a tie-breaking vote.

Yvonne had had no such luck, and so she'd asked for Thomas's help on this vote. Yet she hadn't expected him to make an appearance—not when he could have simply phoned in with his vote.

"Please, sit down," Yvonne said, gesturing to the couch and seating herself. "Before we talk about

church business, I want to know how you've been doing." It had been months since they'd caught up, and
she was eager to hear about his speaking ministry
and his family.

Thomas unbuttoned his suit jacket and sat down
on the couch next to Yvonne. "So, what do you want
to know?"

"For starters, you haven't been traveling as much
lately. Has the world received all the motivation it
needs?"

Thomas laughed. "I'm still getting more requests
for speaking engagements than I can accept, but I
guess I've kind of lost my wanderlust."

Yvonne knew that for years, Brenda had asked
Thomas to spend less time on the road and more time
at home. It seemed strange that now, more than two
years after her death, he was finally willing to limit his
travels. "What brought this on?" she asked.

"Since Brenda died, I've spent a lot of time putting
things into perspective. I want to have time to recon-
nect with my son, which is going to be hard since he
has his own career now."

Yvonne understood exactly where Thomas was
coming from. She and David had spent many years on
the preaching circuit, and then, one day, they looked
up and saw that Toya and Tia were grown. She wished
that she could take credit for the woman Toya had
become, and she definitely wished that she had spent
more time helping Tia mature. If life didn't turn out
right for Tia, Yvonne knew she'd be tempted to blame
herself. "I should have spent more time with my girls
as they were growing up, too." She slapped her hand
against her thigh as she sat up a bit straighter. "But,
hey, I figure I'll get a second chance when they give me
some grandchildren."

"Speak for yourself, Granny," Thomas said, nudging her arm. "I'm not trying to become a poppa for at least another five years. We didn't have Jarrod until I was thirty, so I figure he can at least return the favor and not have his first kid until he's thirty, maybe even thirty-five."

Yvonne chuckled, then laughed outright, so hard that she doubled over. When she finally regained composure, she sat up again and wiped the tears from her eyes. "Okay, maybe I don't want to be a granny so soon, either."

"You certainly don't look like any granny I know. I mean, look at you. You're fifty-two, but you don't look a day over forty."

Yvonne had been told that her looks were what Olay would want in a model to advertise its facial products. Fifty was definitely the new forty where she was concerned. People often said that with her long, coal-black hair, light skin, and eyes that sparkled and danced, she could pass for a relative of Lena Horne. "We've known each other entirely too long. There's no way you should know my real age."

Thomas lifted his hands in surrender. "Don't worry about it. I'll take your secrets to the grave with me."

Yvonne felt her droll mood depart. "I don't want to hear anything about you going to your grave."

Thomas put an arm around Yvonne's shoulder and gave her a squeeze. "I shouldn't have said that. I'm sorry."

With his arm still wrapped around her, Yvonne took a deep breath to steady her nerves. She had seen two deaths too many in the past two years, and she didn't know if she could make it through funeral number three anytime soon. With David and Brenda gone, Yvonne felt that she had fulfilled her quota of homegoings for a lifetime. "Don't say stuff like that. I don't consider it funny."

"Again, I'm sorry," Thomas said as he stood up. "Are you ready for the meeting tomorrow morning?"

Yvonne shook her head and leaned back in the couch. "I've been in ministry for thirty years, copastored Christ-Life for twenty, and now some board that my husband and I formed wants to vote me out. I don't know how to get ready for something like that."

"But I'm here to cast my vote in favor of you staying senior pastor of Christ-Life," Thomas reminded her. "And I believe several others will vote in your favor, also."

Yvonne pushed herself to her feet and planted a kiss on Thomas's cheek. "God love you for what you're doing, Thomas. But I don't know how much good it's going to do. If Deacon Brown has his way, I might need to take on a few of those speaking engagements you've had to turn down."

"Don't worry," Thomas said. "This meeting is in the Lord's hands. He knows that you're meant to pastor this church, and I plan to do everything in my power to make the other board members realize that."

Chapter Two

AT HOME THAT NIGHT, YVONNE FOUND HERSELF REVIEW-ing Scriptures on faith. She desperately needed to trust that God had a plan that would get her out of the jam she was in. In times of doubt, she always opened her Bible and relied on the Word of God to boost her faith. She turned to the eighth chapter of Luke and began to read one of her favorite Scriptures, starting with the eighth verse.

> *Now it happened, on a certain day, that He got into a boat with His disciples. And He said to them, "Let us cross over to the other side of the lake." And they launched out. But as they sailed He fell asleep. And a windstorm came down on the lake, and they were filling with water, and were in jeopardy. And they came to Him and awoke Him, saying, "Master, Master, we are perishing!" Then He arose and rebuked the wind and the raging of the water. And they ceased, and there was a calm. But He said to them, "Where is your faith?" And they were afraid, and marveled, saying to one another, "Who can this be? For He commands even the winds and water, and they obey Him!"*

Right now, rather than calming the wind and water, Yvonne needed the Lord to calm the deacons, elders, church board members, and congregation so that they didn't hastily decide to throw her out. How had things gotten so out of control since David's death? Yvonne simply didn't understand. She had been copastor of Christ-Life for more than two decades and had always been treated kindly and respectfully by the leadership and the members.

Yvonne was turning the pages of her Bible to another favorite passage when her phone rang. She did not like to answer her phone when she was studying her Bible or praying, but when she glanced at the caller ID and saw that it was Tia, she had to pick up. Her younger daughter had daily "drama" in her life, and Yvonne was afraid not to answer the phone. If someone was holding her baby girl hostage, and Tia had managed to break away and call for help, Yvonne would never forgive herself for not taking the call. Tia's drama seemed that extreme at times.

"Hey, honey! How are you doing?" Yvonne tried to sound upbeat, hoping that her drama queen would follow suit.

"Oh, Mama, I'm so sorry," Tia said with a shaking voice.

It was obvious to Yvonne that Tia was crying. She moved her Bible off her lap and sat up. "What's wrong, baby?"

Sniffling, Tia said, "I just wanted you to know how sorry I am about all of this."

If Yvonne had known that Tia would take tomorrow's board meeting to heart like this, she never would have told her about it. She never wanted her daughters to think poorly of Christ-Life Sanctuary or of any of its members or leadership. "Honey, don't worry about me. Your uncle Thomas is in town, and he will be at the meeting. So, I know that I'll have at least one vote on my side."

"That's awesome, Mama. I'm so glad that Uncle Thomas is going to help you with those crabby board members." Tia sniffled again. "But that's not what I'm sorry about."

Drama, drama, drama. Bracing herself, Yvonne said, "I'm listening."

"Before I go any further, I need for you to understand that I never meant for anything like this to happen. And I'm so, so sorry."

"I get that, Tia. You've already told me how sorry you are. So, can you please just tell me what's going on?"

With a burst of fresh tears, Tia blurted out, "I'm pregnant."

Yvonne moved the phone away from her head, looked at it, and then pressed the receiver against her ear again. "Is this your idea of a joke, Tia? Because, if it is, I am not in the mood for this right now."

"I wish I were joking, Mama, but...but it's true," Tia sobbed.

Nothing that Tia had ever done could have prepared Yvonne for this phone call. Not the time when she'd had to pick up her teenage daughter at the police station for mouthing off to a police officer after he'd cited her friend for driving without a license. Not the time when Tia had informed her and David that she was dropping out of college to attend art school in Chicago, where she lived now. And not even the time when Tia had arranged to meet a guy she'd met on the Internet, only to find out that he was an online predator looking for teenage girls to do ungodly things with. No, as shocking as those incidents had been, none of them had prepared Yvonne for this moment.

Tia had always been the "problem child," the one who required a little more time and attention to keep her on the right path—or, when she strayed from the path, to drag her, kicking and screaming, back on track. David had known exactly how to handle her. He would see her hanging with the wrong crowd or chasing after useless things and would instantly redirect her.

Tia had seemed to receive correction from her father better than she received it from her mother, so Yvonne had simply stepped aside and allowed David to discipline their wayward child while she stayed on her knees, praying and interceding for her, as well as for Toya. But whom could she turn to now? She had just confessed to Thomas that she wasn't ready to be a grandmother, and then Tia had the audacity to make her enter granny-land, anyway. *Lord Jesus, I need Your help!* she prayed silently before responding, "Didn't I warn you about dating a guy who is not the least bit interested in the God you serve?" She knew that Tia's commitment to the Lord had wavered in recent years, but using her faith as a platform for punishment seemed like a safe route.

"Robbie is interested in God," Tia insisted. "We talk about the Bible all the time."

Yvonne sighed deeply. "How can you be pregnant, Tia? You're only twenty-four, and…and you're not married."

"I know, b-but Robbie loves me, and—and he w-wants us to get m-married." Tia was crying harder now.

Take a deep breath, Yvonne told herself. *The deed has already been done. This is no time to remind her that she shouldn't be having sex before marriage.* "If Robbie wants to get married, that's a good thing, right?"

"Y-yes.…"

"Then why are you crying so hard?"

"Because...because I didn't want to get married like this. I'm going to be fat walking down the aisle!"

Yvonne glanced at her Bible and wished she had spent the past half hour reading Scriptures on patience rather than faith. "Tia, you're about to bring an innocent life into this world—a life that you neither planned for nor are prepared for. And you're telling me that the thing you're worried about most is being fat at your wedding?"

"That's not all," Tia said defensively. "I'm also upset because I don't have a father to walk me down the aisle."

Yvonne could understand that. She could remember David talking with their girls about how any boys they brought home needed to be respectable Christians, and how, if they knew what was right, they would ask his blessing before proposing to his daughters.... She found that she couldn't respond to Tia's last comment because now she felt like crying, too.

"Oh, Mama!" Tia said with sudden excitement in her voice. "Do you think Uncle Thomas would walk me down the aisle?"

David was supposed to be here for this. He was supposed to walk her down the aisle. He was supposed to hold Yvonne's hand and tell her that everything would be okay.

Yvonne wiped at a runaway tear. "I'll ask him."

Early the next morning, Thomas got in his car and headed for Flint, Michigan. He'd made plans to meet his son for breakfast before the board meeting. At twenty-seven, Jarrod Reed was already a successful sales manager for a Fortune 500 company with locations all over the United States. The job paid well, and Jarrod seemed happy, but Thomas worried that he traveled too much.

As if you have room to talk, he thought to himself, considering that, until recently, he'd traveled almost nonstop—not just throughout the U.S., but also in other countries, as he'd gone from one speaking engagement or book signing to the next. This had been his schedule throughout Jarrod's childhood, and his son had often complained about his long absences from home. Thomas had repeatedly promised that he would slow down someday soon and stop traveling as much so that he, Brenda, and Jarrod could do all the things they'd been planning to do. Too bad "someday soon" had come after Brenda died.

Thomas enjoyed his career. He loved to travel, so having speaking engagements in one town after the next never bothered him, aside from the regret of being away from his family. He'd written twelve best sellers that readers seemed to benefit from. And he liked to believe that he was doing a lot to further the kingdom of Christ. He hadn't been a pastor in over twenty years, but he still delivered the good news to anyone and everyone who attended his workshops and conferences. He spoke on such topics as how to have a fulfilling life with God in the very center of everything. For the last twenty-five years, Thomas had been training pastors, leaders, and congregants, helping them to identify the passion that drives them and live lives of integrity.

Yes, Thomas had accomplished a great deal, but that didn't erase the regret he felt at not having spent enough time with Brenda and Jarrod. It was too late to make amends for being an absentee husband. He hoped, however, that Jarrod would be willing to give his father another chance to be a part of his life.

As Thomas pulled into the parking lot of the restaurant where he was meeting Jarrod, he said a silent prayer, asking God to help him and his son get back the things they'd lost while he was out making a name for himself.

Thomas got out of his car and spotted his son. He was standing outside the restaurant with his back toward Thomas, engaged in what appeared to be a deep conversation with a pretty young woman wearing five-inch heels and a very, very short skirt. Thomas never got too excited about the outward appearance of a woman, because he knew that the inward package was much more important. But he couldn't remember having had a conversation with his son about what to look for in a woman. He walked up and patted Jarrod on the back. "Hey, son! I hope you haven't been waiting on me for too long."

Jarrod turned and shook his hand. "Hey! It was no problem," he said. "I met Marissa while I was waiting, and I was just about to ask her to have breakfast with us."

Spoken like a man with his mind already made up about the woman in front of him, Thomas thought. Well, his mind was made up, too. The woman's blouse was so tight, he thought for sure the buttons were going to burst. "Maybe some other time, son," Thomas said. "I haven't seen you in a while, and I was really looking forward to catching up with you." He then turned to Marissa. "Would you mind giving my son your telephone number so he can give you a call later?"

Marissa smiled, then reached into her purse and pulled out a piece of paper and a pen. "I can do that." She scribbled on the paper and handed it to Jarrod. "Call me when you get a chance."

"I'll talk to you soon, Marissa," Jarrod said, waving as she walked away. He then turned to Thomas. "Where'd you find that car?"

Thomas beamed as he turned to look at his 1947 Buick Roadmaster. "Oh, I bought it at an auction several months ago." All his life, he had admired classic cars but hadn't had the money to do anything about it. That was until ten years ago, when his ministry had kicked into overdrive. He now had three classic cars and was on the hunt for a fourth.

"So, when am I going to get to drive this one?" Jarrod asked. He had developed the same love for classic cars, even though he had yet to purchase one.

Thomas merely chuckled.

"Well, shall we go in?" Jarrod asked.

"Sounds good. I'm starving."

"Mama used to say that you were always starving," Jarrod joked as he held the door for Thomas.

"That was because your mama could cook like nobody I've ever known." Just thinking about the meals Brenda used to prepare made his stomach growl. "That woman could throw down in the kitchen. Now, that's what you need—a woman who can cook. Have you dated any of the women at your church?"

"A few, but I'm not really worried about finding a woman who can cook. Right now, I'm just looking for someone who fits me. You feel me?"

"Oh, I feel you, all right. But trust me, when you marry that woman, you'll be much happier if she shines in the kitchen. A lot of these young girls nowadays know how to throw a TV dinner in the microwave, and that's about it."

Jarrod got a faraway look in his eyes. "Mama always wanted your meals at home to be special. She said that you ate out so much and enjoyed so many meals prepared by top chefs that she didn't want you to feel like you were missing something at home."

Thomas hadn't known that Brenda had gone to all that trouble because she hadn't wanted him to be disappointed with how her cooking compared to restaurant fare. He'd simply thought that she enjoyed preparing elaborate meals. His son's words caught him off guard, and he pondered them as he and Jarrod followed the waitress to their table.

When they were seated, Thomas picked up his menu and began to scan the items as he asked, "Why would your mama think that I would prefer restaurant food to hers?"

"I think Mama wasted a lot of time doing things that you never even noticed. I think she even made herself sick on occasion just to keep you home. But it never worked. You were always back on the road, headed here and there—anywhere but home to your family."

Thomas put down his menu and looked at Jarrod. "I'm sorry, son. There was a time in my life when I had it all wrong. I thought that I had to make a success of myself to make up for failing at pastoring a church. But I never took the time to consider how my need for success was affecting you and your mama."

Jarrod shrugged.

"I know it's too late to make it up to your mama, but if you'd allow me, I'd like to make it up to you."

"How are you going to do that, Dad? I mean, I'm twenty-seven; I don't have any more school field trips for you to chaperone. And if I want to go to Disney World now, I can just take myself."

"I know you can take yourself wherever you want to go. But would you really mind if I tagged along from time to time?"

"How are you going to tag along with me when you have so many commitments to fulfill?"

The waitress came back to the table and asked if they were ready to order.

"Can you give us a few minutes?" Thomas asked her, then turned back to Jarrod. "I have slowed down a bit since your mama passed. I guess I finally realized that I don't have anything to prove to anybody."

Jarrod leaned back in his chair and smiled. "I'm glad that you've finally decided to slow down. I mean, you are getting up there in age, you know?"

"I bet I can still take you in some one-on-one."

"Whatever, old man. Please. Don't even make me embarrass you on the court."

"So, what do you say, Jarrod? I'm here with hat in hand. Do you think you can give your old man a chance?"

"Dad, calm down, okay? I might need a little therapy because of all the time you spent away from home, but I always knew that you loved me. You made that very clear. And I always knew that you were working and traveling to provide for me and Mama. So, I'm not mad at you. And, yeah, I'd like for you to hang out with me from time to time."

"Thanks, kid. Now, about this girl you were talking to outside—"

"Don't even start. You are the last one who should give out any type of advice on relationships," Jarrod told him with a laugh.

That stung. But what could he say? He hadn't been home enough to show Jarrod how to build a lasting relationship with a woman. If anything, Brenda had shown Jarrod more about love than he ever had.

"Can I give you a piece of advice, Dad?" Jarrod asked.

"Sure, son."

"If you ever get married again, please try to be more tuned in to the needs of your wife. Okay?"

Thomas chuckled. "I don't think you have to worry about that, son. I was married to your mama for so long that I can't see myself with anyone else."

"Dad, it's okay with me if you get married again. Honest. I just want you to make the next woman happy."

Thomas grinned, feeling humbled. When he had pulled up and seen his son talking to that woman, he had been worried about his son's choices. But Jarrod was a wise young man. He could teach his father a few things.

Chapter Three

*G*OD HAD OPENED DOORS FOR YVONNE EARLY IN HER ministry. Once word had spread about Yvonne Milner's life-changing messages, she had been invited to preach at numerous churches in the local area. Then, the list of invitations had grown even more numerous and covered a much larger region. In her early years, she'd preached messages on holiness and repentance in the spirit of Reverend Jackie McCullough. But even though she had been in high demand, those early years had been challenging because of the way women preachers were treated. When Yvonne first began traveling from church to church to preach, she often encountered people who informed her that she was not allowed to enter the pulpit. Instead, a portable podium would be brought down to the floor, and she would have to deliver her message from there.

There were times when Yvonne felt like storming out of the church in protest, but the Lord would always admonish her to stay. So, Yvonne would humbly deliver the message the Lord had given her and then thank the people in attendance.

But as the years passed, a new movement took hold in the church. Pastors' wives began organizing women's conferences, events that brought in some of the most respected women in ministry to encourage and build up the women of the church. As those conferences started to flourish, certain male pastors who coveted their pulpits so much that they forbade women to stand behind them began to sit up and take notice. Once the women's conference movement took off, Yvonne never had to stand on the floor to preach again. Many pulpits were open and welcoming to male and female preachers alike. But now it felt as if Yvonne's own congregation was trying to relegate her to the floor again.

At first, she had felt deeply hurt and more than a little angry at the church board members for turning their backs on her. After hearing Tia's confession, however, Yvonne was half tempted to sit her own self down and hand her position to someone else. Her eyes had been opened to the truth: she loved sharing the gospel and was filled with joy every time a repentant heart turned to God. But she had been so busy grieving David's death that she had lost that joy and had been doing her job as if it was just that—a job, rather than a ministry. Yvonne could now admit that she hadn't been an effective leader of her church, and she hadn't been an attentive mother, either. She understood why the board wanted her to resign. She was hindering the growth of the church she claimed to love. But did she love it enough to do the right thing? And just what was the right thing?

She sighed and sat down at the head of the conference table to wait for the board members to come in and pronounce judgment against her. *If only David were here, she thought. He would know what to do.* But wasn't that the reason she was in so much hot water now—because David wasn't here and would never be here again? She had let her husband's death steal her joy, and she'd taken her focus off of building the ministry the two of them had labored together to grow for so many years.

Yvonne had to face the facts. David was gone, and she was driving Christ-Life Sanctuary into the ground. She couldn't imagine that God was pleased with the way she had been handling things. Since David's death, she had scheduled countless ministers to preach on Sunday mornings when she'd known full well that the congregation was expecting to hear from her. She'd cancelled retreats and conferences that many members looked forward to each year. She had been grieving too much to think about what mattered to her church members. No wonder so many people had chosen to leave after David's death.

She hadn't even been there for her own daughters these past eighteen months. Toya was strong. She could survive while Yvonne took time to grieve. But Tia needed her mother, and, in the absence of her care and support, her baby had gotten pregnant and was now expecting a baby of her own. Yvonne couldn't let it end like this. From this day forward, by the grace of God, she would strive to be a better mother. And if the church board would give her another chance, she would be the leader God had ordained her to be. Her destiny was tied to this church. David might be dead, but God's church was still very much alive, albeit languishing. Yvonne would never again be responsible for its failure to thrive.

The door to the conference room opened, and Deacon Clarence Brown walked in. He was the church's finance director, as well as a member of the board. Deacon Brown didn't want a woman telling him how to get from here to there, let alone how to live his life.

Yvonne knew that he was opposed to her primarily because he didn't want a woman preaching to him about anything. But she had known this man for years; she and David had often invited him over for dinner, and they'd attended his children's college graduations and weddings. So, Yvonne hoped that Deacon Brown would change his mind about her.

"Pastor," Deacon Brown said, acknowledging Yvonne as he sat down next to her.

"Hey, Deacon. I hope you're in a better mood today," Yvonne said, hoping humor would convince him that she'd forgiven his behavior from the last time she'd talked to him. The time he'd flat out accused her of driving members away from the church.

Deacon Brown had sense enough to lower his head in apparent regret. "Things got a little out of hand during our last meeting, Pastor," he said. "I assure you, I meant no disrespect."

Before Yvonne could respond to him, the door opened again, and, one by one, elders Dwight Conrad, Wanda Pearson, Beverly Carson, and Joel Johnson came in. They took their seats, and their efforts not to look in her direction were obvious to Yvonne. These people had been her friends, her confidants, and she wasn't about to let this meeting take away the good memories she'd made with them. "Hello, everyone," she said, trying to sound cheerful. "I'm glad you could make it."

Somehow, all of the board members seemed to have caught the lowered-head disease. They mumbled their hellos or spoke to her while appearing to examine the carpet beneath the table.

Yvonne was saved from having to manufacture further conversation with people who obviously didn't want to talk with her when Thomas walked into the conference room. She smiled as every head in the room turned to him. Thomas had a commanding presence, whether he was dressed in jeans and a T-shirt or an expensive tailored suit like the one he wore now. But then again, Yvonne reasoned, it would be hard not to notice a six-foot-three-inch, hundred-and-eighty-pound chocolate treat like Thomas. *Oh my gosh! Did I really just think that?* Yvonne silently chided herself for her thoughts. She had known Thomas for more than thirty years, so, naturally, she'd noticed that the man was handsome; that was a fact that no man, woman, or child could ignore. But she had never thought of him as a "chocolate treat"!

Okay, she needed to rewind and refocus. This was an important meeting concerning her place in the ministry that she and her husband had built. It was certainly not the time to be thinking about how handsome some guy was. She cleared her throat and, when she believed she had everyone's attention, whether they were looking at her or not, she began. "Okay, since everyone is here now, I guess we can get this meeting started."

Almost before she'd finished speaking, Deacon Brown stood up. "None of us wants to be here," he said, letting his gaze fall on each person at the table. "We all recognize that Pastor Yvonne helped build this church right alongside Pastor David. And we're grateful for everything she's done for this ministry through the years."

Then, why are we here? Yvonne wanted to ask. But she was sure that Deacon Brown was getting ready to fill them all in on the reason this cutthroat meeting had been called.

"Now, Pastor Yvonne, we know that you've been under a lot of stress since Pastor David passed away. You've done the best you could, considering the circumstances, but the fact remains that we are losing members left and right—"

"You blame me for the members leaving the church?" Yvonne interrupted him. This was a sore subject for her, and as much as she was trying to practice self-restraint and remain cool, she could not help defending herself. She had nurtured and cared for so many of Christ-Life's members through the years, and the fact that many of them had just walked out at a time when she desperately needed them didn't sit right with her. The intimation that their departure had been her own fault was not something she wanted to hear right now, as much as she acknowledged its validity. She looked around the table at the faces of the men and women, some of whom had been handpicked by her to serve on this board. None of them met her eyes.

There was a moment of awkward silence, during which Deacon Brown sat down again, and then Elder Dwight spoke. "We know things have been difficult for you, Pastor Yvonne. And God knows we don't want to make things worse."

"But not only have we lost members; we are now in debt to the tune of three hundred thousand dollars, with no way to pay our creditors," Deacon Brown chimed in.

"And I guess the tanking economy is my fault, too?" Yvonne felt herself glaring at the board members, daring them to blame her. "Is it my fault, Deacon Brown, that so many of our members have lost their jobs in the auto industry and now don't have enough money to put in the offering plate?"

When no one responded, Yvonne was tempted to start doling out pieces of her mind as if she were passing out candy. One by one, she wanted to let the board members know just what she thought of their scheming. God doesn't like ugly, and right now, Yvonne wished for warts and big fat pimples to cover their faces—sparing Thomas, of course. She wanted them to be just as ugly on the outside as they clearly had to be on the inside.

"I can tell that you're upset, Pastor, but you need to look at this thing from our perspective," Deacon Brown finally replied. "The bank is bound to foreclose on this church building in a couple of months if we don't come up with the money we owe, and with the rate at which members are leaving the church, it doesn't seem like we'll ever be able to catch up on these bills."

"Okay," Yvonne conceded. "I may not have been attuned to the effect my grieving was having on the growth of the church. But I'm only human. If you guys give me a chance, I know I can fix this."

Elder Joel Johnson spoke up next. "To be honest, Pastor, we've given you eighteen months too long already. I don't think this church can survive with you at the helm for much longer."

Elder Johnson's statement hurt like a punch in the stomach. Yvonne wanted to defend herself. She wanted to list off all the things she had personally done for this church. But then she remembered Tia's call with the news that she was pregnant. She also thought about how many times she had declined to preach because she had been too busy grieving. And she relented.

"Look, I didn't come here to argue with you all. The fact is, I agree with your conclusions." At that moment, she wanted to resign and save them the trouble of throwing her out of the church she'd helped her husband build, but she couldn't bring herself to say the words. So, she decided to just let them do it. They seemed eager enough to be rid of her. "Let's just go ahead and vote."

She glanced at Thomas, who gave her a look that begged her not to throw in the towel. "Are you sure about this, Yvonne?"

Yvonne turned away. She couldn't bear to look into his eyes. She knew he didn't want her to give up so easily, but what else could she do? The board members were right. She hadn't just been neglecting aspects of the job; she hadn't acknowledged her grief and dealt with it constructively, and so she hadn't done her job, period. God help her, she wished she could change things, because she didn't want to be forced out of her beloved church. But if she was running it to the ground, how could she stay? "I don't think they are interested in anything I have to say, so we might as well get on with it," she told him.

Thomas's heart broke at the sadness he saw in Yvonne's eyes. Looking around the room at the stern faces of most of the other board members, he could tell that this vote was not going to go well. He couldn't let them take this church from Yvonne. Moved by an inner urging that could only have been the Spirit, he stood up and announced, "There is no need to hold a vote. I will give Christ-Life Sanctuary the three hundred thousand it needs to clear its debt."

"B-but w-why would you do that?" Elder Conrad sputtered.

"Good grief, man, who cares why?" Elder Johnson said. "If Thomas is willing to get our necks out of the noose, I'm just going to accept his money and say thank you." He smiled for the first time since he'd entered the conference room.

"In good conscience, I can't let you do this, Mr. Reed," Deacon Brown said. "This church is deep in debt. You'd be throwing your money away."

"It's my money. I should be able to 'throw it' wherever I want," Thomas countered.

He glanced at Yvonne, who stared at him with an expression of disbelief on her face. He nodded to assure her that he knew what he was doing, but she didn't look convinced.

"Deacon Brown is right, Thomas," she said. "If the church is in this much debt, and our tithing members are leaving, how can I hope to guarantee that you will get your money back?"

"Well, doesn't the Bible say that it is more blessed to give than to receive? I believe the Word of God, so I'll just give you the money. There's no need to give it back."

Now Yvonne stood up, placed her palms firmly on the table, and leaned forward toward Thomas. "I will not let you do this," she said firmly. "Go give your money to Jarrod if you have three hundred thousand dollars to throw away. Let him buy a Ferrari with it or something."

"Well, there's where you're wrong, Yvonne, because I'm not just throwing my money away. The money I'm offering to Christ-Life Sanctuary comes with conditions." Thomas had another nudge from the Spirit, and he was certain that this would convince the board members.

"And what are your conditions, Mr. Reed?" Elder Beverly Carson asked.

"I have only two. The first condition: Yvonne must be allowed to stay on as pastor of Christ-Life." He paused for a silent prayer for confirmation. "And the second condition: I will become copastor."

"Thomas Reed, have you lost your mind?" Yvonne asked as she closed the door after ushering the last of the board members out of the conference room.

"No, I haven't."

"Then, why on earth would you tell those people that you want to pastor a church?"

"It shut them up, didn't it? Just minutes ago, they were stone-faced and ready to kick you out of your own church. Then, after I spoke up, they were congratulating us and wishing us well as they happily bounced out of here."

Yvonne folded her arms across her chest. "And what do you think they are going to do when they realize that you never really intended to move to Detroit or to pastor a dying ministry?"

"Who says I'm not moving to Detroit? My son lives nearby, and he and I are trying to work on our relationship. Oh, and I've got one more reason to move to Detroit: my new church is here. So, what's the problem?"

"You don't like being tied down, Thomas. That's the problem." Yvonne unfolded her arms and rubbed her temples. "Look, Thomas. I know you want to help me, but I don't want you to be miserable in the process."

"Who says I would be miserable? I already told you, I've reached a point in my life where I'm tired of traveling. I've always been in ministry, except that mine has been more on the road. Now I want to grow some roots. I can help you rebuild this church, Yvonne. I'm the one who got you into this mess in the first place, remember?" He gave her a sheepish grin.

Yvonne smiled begrudgingly. He was mostly right. Thomas had been the one to convince David that a woman could be called to preach the gospel just as easily as a man—an argument Yvonne had tried to make for years, but to no avail. Then, Thomas had come to Christ-Life Sanctuary and preached at a Sunday morning service. Yvonne hadn't attended that morning, because one of her daughters had been ill, but when David had come home afterward, he'd broken down and cried in front of her. He'd asked her to forgive him and told her that he would never again stand in the way of what God was doing in her life. Yvonne was grateful that Thomas had preached the message God had given him to deliver that morning. But that was no reason for her to continue using this man.

"I'm offering my help to you, Yvonne. Please, take it."

"All I asked for was your vote, Thomas. I didn't ask for your money, and I didn't ask you to commit your life to something to fulfill my dreams."

"I know that, Yvonne. But I really believe that God is pulling me this way. He has been readjusting things in my life lately and helping me to see the error of my ways." He took her hands and gave them a squeeze. "You need help with this church, Yvonne. Let me be the one to help you."

She closed her eyes for a moment to collect her thoughts, then opened them again and met his gaze.

"You have always been there for David and me, Thomas, and for that, I am forever grateful. But I can't ask you to throw the rest of your life away on me. I just can't."

"I wouldn't be throwing my life away. I want to do this, Yvonne. Won't you at least think about it?"

She pulled her hands out of his and lowered herself into a chair, propping her elbows on the conference table with her palms up. "What do you know about running a church? The first one you had flopped. That's why you went out on the road, remember?" Even though Yvonne realized that Thomas might be hurt by her words, she was determined to give him a wake-up call.

"I remember. But do you remember why my churched flopped?" Without giving her time to answer, Thomas continued, "Because I was too proud to accept help. David offered to help alleviate our debt, but my belief was that the Lord should take care of everything, and if He didn't, then He didn't want me to be a pastor. But I was wrong, Yvonne." He sat down across from her and put his hands over hers. "We can make this work, Yvonne. You just have to trust me."

Yvonne squirmed in her seat. He really wasn't giving up, was he? "I—I don't know, Thomas."

"Will you at least go out to lunch with me so we can talk about this?"

She'd gone to lunch with Thomas a hundred times. He was her friend, and she needed a friend right now. "Okay, let's do lunch. But no more of this crazy talk."

Chapter Four

WHILE YVONNE WAS DRIVING HOME TO CHANGE HER clothes and freshen up before lunch with Thomas, Toya called her on her cell phone. "Hey, Toy-Toy," Yvonne said when she picked up the phone. She'd given Toya the nickname as a child, and she wondered if she'd ever stop using it.

"Uncle Thomas saves the day again! I'm telling you, Mama, that man was born to be your hero."

"Calm down, Toya. Thomas isn't going to be a hero for anybody, because I'm not letting him do this. And how do you know what happened at the board meeting, anyway?"

"Beverly Carson called me. She said that Uncle Thomas stood up and started throwing his money around and then told everybody just how things were going to be done from now on."

Beverly worked at the law firm where Toya was an attorney, and she was a big blabbermouth. That go-tell-it-on-the-mountain mouth of Beverly's made most sisters in the church careful to keep their business to themselves. "I think Thomas just panicked," Yvonne rationalized. "He's trying to help me keep the church, and I think he felt like we were running out of options, so he just blurted out the first thing that came to mind without talking to me first."

"Well, it sounds like it worked. Beverly told me that the board had already decided that no matter what you said, they were voting you out, but when Uncle Thomas said he would pay off the debt and help you pastor the church, they were willing to reconsider."

"Well, wasn't that nice of them?" Yvonne cringed at her oozing sarcasm but continued, anyway. "Do you think they realize that Thomas is a man who will never be able to settle in one place? He has to be on the go. How can he pastor a church if he's never here?"

Toya gave an exasperated sigh. "You need to let Uncle Thomas worry about that, Mama. You need him right now, and the sooner you accept that fact and deal with reality, the better."

"And what is reality as you see it, Toya?"

"Whether you want to admit it or not, the reality of your situation is that your board members think you are a hazard to the health of Christ-Life Sanctuary. And without Uncle Thomas, you wouldn't have a chance at staying senior pastor. Now, I know this isn't fair. There are extenuating circumstances that your congregation doesn't seem to care about."

"That's right. My husband died. I miss the man."

"I know. We all do. Daddy was an awesome man and a respected pastor. But it's been almost two years, Mama. You've got to find a way to stop allowing your grief to consume you and move on with your life. And I believe that is the message your board wanted to send to you today."

"What are you saying, Toya?"

"I just think you should accept help when you need it. You're a strong woman. I get that. But even Jesus needed the disciples to help Him through His journey on earth."

That was her Toya, always the practical one. If something was broken, then it needed to be fixed. Plain and simple. But Yvonne didn't want to take advantage of her friendship with Thomas or feel like she was using him and his generosity. "I appreciate what Thomas is trying to do, Toya, and I admit that I've dug myself into a hole that I need help getting out of. But if I decide to accept Thomas's help, it will have to be a temporary thing. I'm not trying to take the man's money or his nomadic spirit away from him."

"All right, Mama. You do what you think is best, and I'll be praying for you."

"Thank you, sweetie. I need all the prayers I can get right now." *Not only for this board meeting, but also to know what to do about Tia.* She assumed that Toya had yet to learn about Tia's pregnancy, and she decided that Tia could tell her sister herself. "Talk to you later, okay?"

"Okay. Love you!"

"I love you, too."

They hung up just as Yvonne pulled into her driveway. She went inside, took a shower, and then dressed for lunch.

Yet before she could leave the house, her phone rang again. She was tempted not to answer it, but the caller ID displayed Tia's name. "Hey, hon. I'm on my way out—can I call you when I'm in the car?"

"Mama, I really need to talk to you—now!" Tia screamed. She sounded hysterical.

Oh, Lord, what could have happened to this child now? Yvonne sat down on the couch, figuring that whatever was wrong would take no more than a minute for Tia to explain. "What's the matter, sweetie? What happened?"

"Robbie lost his job."

"What? Why?"

"His boss says he showed up to work drunk."

"Are you telling me that Robbie has a drinking problem?" Yvonne was floored. Although she didn't get to talk with Robbie often, since he and Tia lived in Chicago, she had met him several times and had never gotten the sense that he was a drinker.

"No, Mama. Robbie doesn't have a drinking problem. He had a bad cold, so he took some cold medicine and went to work. I guess the medicine made him a little woozy, and he was driving the forklift erratically. His boss got upset and accused him of being drunk, but all he was trying to do was feel better so he could work."

"Fighting a cold or not, Robbie never should have been driving that forklift if he was medicated. His boss was right to be angry. Someone could have been seriously injured."

"Yeah, but now Robbie and I won't have money to pay our bills."

That's my Tia, always thinking of others first. "Looks to me like Robbie needs to be out looking for another job. And maybe this time he won't take so much cold medicine—if that is, in fact, what he took." Yvonne knew she sounded harsh, but she wanted to believe she could expect more from the father of her future grandchild.

"Did you ask Uncle Thomas if he would walk me down the aisle?" Tia asked, changing the subject.

"Not yet, honey, but I'm meeting him for lunch. I'll ask him then."

"Why didn't you ask him earlier? You know how much Uncle Thomas travels. If you wait much longer, he might be all booked up."

I was a little busy trying to keep my own job, Yvonne wanted to say to her daughter. But she knew that Tia hadn't given a thought that morning to the decisive board meeting. The fact that she had almost been thrown out of the pulpit of her church was of minor importance compared to her little princess' wedding. "I've got to go, Tia. I'll call you tomorrow."

"But I still need to discuss the wedding with you!"

"What do we have to discuss, Tia? The boy doesn't have a job, and I know that you would never marry a man with no job." If there was one thing that Yvonne had tried to instill in her girls, it was 2 Thessalonians 3:10: *"If anyone will not work, neither shall he eat."* Real men took care of their families.

"I'm still pregnant, Mama, so of course I'm going to marry him. Robbie will find another job."

"Let's talk about this tomorrow, all right? I've got to go."

"Okay, but call me first thing in the morning," Tia demanded.

"I will." Yvonne hung up the phone and closed her eyes, trying to clear her mind. She hoped and prayed that Tia knew what she was doing, and that she wasn't making the biggest mistake of her life.

Then, she jumped up off the couch, gathered her purse, and got in her car. When she and Thomas had left the church, they'd agreed to meet at Bourbon Steak in one hour. Now, she was running late, so she sped down the street, trying to make up for lost time. On the highway, she drove twenty miles an hour over the speed limit, praying that no policemen with radar guns were nearby.

No such luck. Flashing lights appeared in her rear-view mirror, and Yvonne's heart sank as she pulled to the side of the road. *Not again.* She had plenty of friends who pulled the "I'm a preacher" card whenever they were pulled over for speeding or other traffic violations. But Yvonne never did that. In her thirty-six years of driving, she'd been caught speeding only two other times. Both times, she'd taken the ticket without argument and dutifully mailed in her payment. So, when the state trooper knocked on her window and asked for her license and registration, Yvonne complied without uttering a word.

The trooper took the information, then leaned down so that his face was level with hers. He wore a big grin. "Pastor Yvonne?"

She immediately recognized him as Charlie Randall, a longtime member of Christ-Life. Hopefully he would keep this incident to himself. "Hey, Charlie! How are you doing?"

"I'm doing good, Pastor Yvonne. My wife still listens to her CDs of the sermons you've preached. She can't wait to buy some new ones."

Since David's death, Yvonne had been preaching about one Sunday a month. And each of those sermons had been delivered halfheartedly. Lately, Yvonne had been appointing various elders to preach most of the sermons, giving the excuse that the elders had been wondering when they would have a chance to preach. But again, Yvonne knew that she had been neglecting her responsibilities.

All that was about to change. Since the board had agreed to give her a second chance, Yvonne felt that she had no choice but to accept Thomas's offer. But she had a few conditions of her own that he would have to live with. "Well, you can tell Marilyn that she won't have to wait much longer, because I will be back in the pulpit full-time starting this Sunday."

Charlie did a little jump. "That's good news, Pastor!" He leaned in closer and lowered his voice. "I'm gonna let you off with just a warning this time, but try to drive a little slower, okay?"

"Thank you, Charlie. I appreciate your kindness. I will slow down, I promise." *And I'm on my way to slow Thomas Reed down, too*, she thought as she pulled away with a wave.

Chapter
Five

℘Y THE TIME YVONNE ARRIVED AT THE RESTAURANT, Thomas had already been seated, and he had an appetizer of Crab Louie lettuce cups waiting on her.

"How did you remember that I liked these things?" she asked as she sat down. "It's been a couple of years since we last ate here."

"How could I forget?" Thomas said as she inhaled the aroma of the lettuce cups, then popped one in her mouth. "You practically hugged those lettuce cups to your chest and wouldn't let the rest of us have any."

Yvonne swallowed. "That was right after Brenda passed. David and I brought you here to cheer you up. I'm sorry if I was uncharitable with the appetizer."

"It's okay. You can make up for it by sharing with me now."

"All right," she said begrudgingly as she pushed the plate closer to him. "Eat as many as you want."

When the server came back to the table, Thomas ordered the sixteen-ounce Kansas City strip with a grilled lobster tail. Yvonne didn't have a taste for steak, so she ordered the king crab legs with a side salad and a baked potato.

While they waited for their food, they reminisced about their early days in ministry and swapped stories about peaks and pitfalls over the years, even if some of those stories were already familiar, if not infamous.

When their meals arrived, Thomas said grace, and then they dug in, continuing their light banter throughout the meal. It felt good to spend time with an old friend, one who knew her past and shared her pain in the loss of a spouse. But as they were finishing up, Thomas leaned toward her and said, "See how comfortable we are with each other? You and I would be good together."

What? His comment caught her off guard, and she must have grimaced terribly, for he quickly held up a hand. "That came out wrong. I meant that we would be good pastoring the church together. The two of us would make a good team."

Yvonne put her fork down and reached out to press Thomas's hand. "We're good friends, Thomas—that's why were so comfortable with each other," she gently explained. "But you know as well as I do that it's hard for friends to work together." The last thing she wanted was to start some venture with Thomas and then lose him as a friend because they were constantly at each other's throats. She had lost too much already.

"We'll be just fine, Yvonne," Thomas insisted.

"You say that now, but I can be hard to deal with. Especially when I think I'm right about an issue."

"Like right now, when you're giving me a hard time, and all I want to do is help a friend out? Come on, Yvonne. I promised David that I would do everything in my power to help if you should ever need me. And, well, you need me now."

Yvonne pressed a hand to her brow and shook her head. What else could she say to make him understand? She lifted her head and looked him in the eye. "I know I need you, but this is too much. I can't take everything you're offering."

"Why not?"

"Because I know you, Thomas. Your heart has never been at home in one place for too long. You're a wanderer...and that's okay. Maybe God gave you that restless spirit so that you would find joy in being on the road so much. Somebody has to take His message all over the world."

"I've done all of that, Yvonne. And I missed so much. I even let my son down by not showing up at the events that were important to him." Thomas shook his head. "I still haven't forgiven myself for how I neglected Brenda and Jarrod. But God is giving me a second chance with Jarrod, and I'm going to take it. Are you going to take your second chance, too?"

"Here's the deal, Thomas. I'm not a fool. So, yes, I'll admit I do need your help to get out of this mess. But if I accept your help, you will have to accept my conditions. Okay?"

Thomas put on his sad-puppy-dog face, then tilted his face heavenward and said, "I offer the woman my money and whatever I can do to help, and she puts conditions on accepting them. Lord, Your children really know how to make a man feel unloved."

Yvonne tried to frown but ended up grinning, instead. "Stop acting crazy. Just listen to my idea."

"Okay. Tell me what you need."

Their server stopped by the table again and asked, "Does anyone want dessert?"

Yvonne patted her stomach. "No, thanks. I couldn't eat another bite."

Thomas shook his head. "I'll just take the check, please."

When the server had gone, Yvonne said, "Okay. I know that you said you're ready to stop traveling so much, but I don't buy it. You may be tired of being on the road right now, but soon enough, you'll get that wanderlust again. And that's fine with me—great, actually. Because I would like you to come to Christ-Life and copastor the church with me...on a temporary basis."

Thomas gave her a quizzical look. "So, what are you saying? Are you putting me on a six-month probation or something?"

"You're not on probation, Thomas. But I want you to be free to be the man God made you to be. I don't want to tie you down and make you unhappy. So, the minute you get the itch to go back on the road, don't let me stop you. I need you to promise me that you will live your life and not get stuck here with me."

Thomas didn't want to go back on the road full-time. And he didn't think that the commitment he was willing to make to Christ-Life Sanctuary would cause him to feel stuck. However, he was starting to feel a bit uneasy about his decision, for a completely different reason from what Yvonne suspected. When he had slipped up and said that he and Yvonne would be "good together," she'd thought he'd meant as a couple. The look of horror on her face had made it clear that she could not bear to even imagine that scenario—and that bothered him more than he would have expected it to.

He and Yvonne had never thought of each other in that manner before, so why should he care if she was repelled by the idea of being with him? It wasn't like he wanted to be with her, anyway...right?

As a matter of fact, Thomas wasn't sure if he wanted to enter into holy matrimony ever again. Although he'd loved Brenda dearly, their marriage had been far from perfect. In the beginning, he'd always invited Brenda to travel with him, but she'd always found an excuse to stay home. Plus, she'd been afraid of planes, trains, automobiles, and just about every other form of transportation. Once Jarrod was born, she'd no longer needed to come up with excuses. She was a stay-at-home mom, and she took her role literally. Jarrod was critical of his father because of how much he believed Brenda had missed him during his trips, but Jarrod never knew that Thomas would have loved for his family to tag along on those trips.

Maybe Yvonne was right. He didn't need to tie himself down to one place and commit himself to a woman who wasn't even his wife. "Okay," Thomas finally said. "Let's do this your way. I'll copastor the church until you can get things back in order, and then I'll get back on the road."

"Thank you, Thomas. You are such a great friend."

Thomas picked up the leather folio the server had just dropped off and slid his credit card into the inside pocket. "Is there anything else I can do that might help?"

"Well, there are two more things I want to discuss."

"Name them. Whatever they are, I'll make them happen for you."

"First, the money you offered was a wonderful gesture, but I can't let you give such a large gift."

"How are you going to pay the bills if you don't take the money?" Thomas asked.

"Oh, I want the money. I just don't want you to *give* it to us. So, I am asking you for a loan. And I'd like you to have your accountant look over our books to ensure that Christ-Life will be a good investment for you."

Thomas rolled his eyes. "Just take the money, Yvonne. We don't have to go through all of that. When my church was in trouble, David offered me money. So, what's the difference?"

"The difference is that you didn't take that money, Thomas Reed, and you know it."

"That's because I was young, stubborn, and full of pride. Don't make my mistakes, Yvonne."

"I said I would take the money, as long as you have your accountant list it as a loan. I don't want to feel like I'm taking money away from Jarrod's inheritance, so please, just make a loan to us, Thomas. Okay?" She extended her hand.

Resignedly, Thomas shook her hand. "You're too stubborn for your own good, you know that?"

Yvonne smiled but didn't respond.

"What was the other thing you wanted to talk to me about?"

"Oh, right. Tia wants you to walk her down the aisle."

Thomas nearly jumped out of his seat. "Little Tia is getting married?" He slammed the table jubilantly. "That girl isn't old enough to be throwing her heart away on some worthless man."

"Oh, you and David are just alike. No man could ever be good enough for Tia or Toya, to hear the two of you tell it. But Tia is pregnant, and—"

"She's *what*?" Thomas hit the table again, this time in anger. "Who is the jerk? I'll break his neck."

"No, you're not going to harm the father of my first grandchild. But you can make sure he knows that there will be no cold feet at this shotgun wedding."

"Done. And tell Tia that I would be honored to walk her down the aisle. When are they getting married?"

"I don't know yet. She just told me about all of this last night."

"And you're not in shock?"

"Oh, I'm in shock, all right, I'm just good at hiding it. Nothing that girl says can surprise me anymore."

Thomas reached across the table and gave her shoulder a squeeze. "It will turn out fine. At least they believe in the importance of the marriage covenant, right?"

Yvonne smiled blandly. "Thank you for doing this for her, Thomas. You are such a good friend to me and to my family, and I never want to lose your friendship."

When the server returned with Thomas's credit card, he filed it back inside his wallet, then stood up and held out a hand for Yvonne. They walked out of the restaurant arm in arm, talking and laughing like a married couple. Thomas hoped that their relationship would be strengthened, not damaged, by their working together to pastor Christ-Life.

Chapter Six

$\mathcal{D}$EACON CLARENCE BROWN SAT BEHIND THE DESK IN his real estate office, opening mail and frowning as he reviewed one delinquency notice after another.

Across from him, Marvel Williams looked at his watch and sighed impatiently. "The church is set to go into foreclosure next month. How soon after that will you be able to convince Pastor Yvonne to sell the building to me?" Marvel asked.

Clarence tried to come up with a time estimate. He hated himself for getting involved with Marvel Williams's scheme, but since Detroit's economy had bottomed out, Clarence's realty company had been taking a slow walk toward bankruptcy. Marvel had offered him a sweet deal if he could get Pastor Yvonne to sell the church building to him. But now that Thomas was putting up money to cover the debt, there was no way Clarence would be able to convince her to sell. "We've run into some problems," Clarence said without looking at Marvel.

"What kind of problems?"

Clarence took a deep breath and lifted his head. "Thomas Reed is putting up the money to pay off the church's debt."

"Who is this Thomas Reed?"

"An old friend of the Milners. But he has the money to pay off the debt, so there won't be any foreclosure."

Marvel unbuttoned the jacket of his two-piece, gray pinstriped suit and leaned in closer. "I saw her out to lunch with some guy yesterday. The two of them appeared to be very comfortable with each other."

"It was probably Thomas. Pastor Yvonne has known him for more than thirty years. He was best friends with her late husband."

Marvel got a glint in his eyes. "Do you think they were fooling around before her husband died?"

The slight frown that had been on Clarence's face was replaced with a scowl. "Look. I might be trying to help you purchase my church building and the land it sits on, but don't for a moment think that I will help you drag Pastor Yvonne's name through the mud. She's a good, godly woman, and I don't appreciate your insinuation that she might have cheated on her husband."

"Spare me the loyalty speech, Brown. Business is business, and if I have to slander your pastor and tarnish her reputation to get what I want, then, guess what? I'm not above doing that."

Clarence leaned back in his seat and studied Marvel. He was a well-dressed, good-looking young man with a confident—no, cocky—air about him. He couldn't be more than thirty, but he had accomplished a lot in his life. Before his twenty-fifth birthday, he'd made his first million, and he hadn't stopped making money since. Marvel could have chosen to build his factory on any side of town he wanted; the mayor of Detroit was behind him because the factory would create new jobs. So, he had decided that he wanted the land where Christ-Life Sanctuary sat, plus all the houses that surrounded the church. He'd also decided that he wanted Toya Milner.

"Have you made any headway with Toya?" Clarence asked him.

"I don't want her to know anything about this until the deed is done," Marvel said firmly.

"I hope you know that Toya is not going to like the fact that you're trying to destroy her mother's church."

"You let me worry about Toya. Besides, I'm willing to pay a fair price for that land. Her mother can build another church in another neighborhood with the money she gets."

With that, Marvel stood up and walked to the door. He opened it, then turned back to Clarence. "Get this thing done already, all right? Don't make me handle it my way. Because if I do, I guarantee you it won't be pretty."

Yvonne gazed at her beautiful daughters, who were sitting in her church office talking about wedding plans. Tia and Toya looked almost like twins. They both had high cheekbones, big brown eyes, and full, "pouty" lips. The salient difference was that Toya was high yellow, like Yvonne, while Tia's complexion was more caramel, like David's had been.

"Do you girls want to take this discussion into the sanctuary?" she asked them.

They stopped talking, and Tia shot her a puzzled look. "Why do we need to do that?"

"So we can decide where you'll put the flowers and the arch."

Shaking her head, Tia said, "Oh no, Mama. We're not having the wedding here."

"What?" Now it was Yvonne's turn to be puzzled. "Why on earth wouldn't you want to have your wedding at Christ-Life?"

"Well, for one thing, the members here are going to judge me for getting pregnant without being married."

Why was her daughter being so unreasonable? This was their home church, not to mention where the mother of the bride was senior pastor. Yvonne turned to her older daughter, hoping for some help. "Toya, can you please talk some sense into your sister?"

"I don't know, Mama. If I had gotten pregnant and wasn't married"—she held up her hands in response to the warning glare Yvonne gave her—"which I would never do, of course, I don't think I'd want to have my wedding here, either."

Yvonne had assumed that they'd planned for this meeting to take place at the church so that they could walk through the sanctuary and come up with ideas for decorations and seating arrangements. She had assumed—foolishly, she realized—that Tia would dance excitedly around the sanctuary while deciding where to set up the bridal arch, the unity candle, and so forth. Instead, her wayward daughter had informed her that she didn't want to get married at Christ-Life. And her sensible daughter agreed with her.

Yvonne sighed. "I don't understand either one of you. This is the church you grew up in. You've been away since you enrolled in art school, Tia, but I always assumed that you would return to this church, at least for your wedding. Was I wrong?"

"I made a mistake, Mama, but I haven't completely lost my faith. I have asked God to forgive me for my sins, and I believe He has. But I just can't take seeing the looks of pity or contempt on everybody's face on what is supposed to be the happiest day of my life."

"It's not the church members' fault that you're pregnant, Tia." Yvonne stood up and walked over to her window. She surveyed the unfinished Family Life Center, then turned back to her daughter. "Many of the people at this church have watched you grow up—some even taught you in their Sunday school classes—and they would be honored to attend your wedding."

Before Tia could respond, there was a knock at the door, and then it opened. Thomas walked in and grinned at Tia and Toya. "I heard that my girls were in here! I couldn't let the two of you get away without giving me a big hug."

Tia and Toya jumped out of their seats and took turns hugging Thomas and giving him a kiss on the cheek.

"I'm so glad that you're here, Uncle Thomas," said Tia, lowering herself onto the edge of Yvonne's desk, where Toya also sat. "I need you to talk to Mama for me."

"What's wrong?" Thomas asked her as he turned toward Yvonne, who folded her arms across her chest and gave him a steady gaze.

"I don't want to have my wedding at the church, and Mama is acting like I'm going to offend the entire church if I get married at another church," Tia whined.

"Getting married elsewhere would offend the members who have watched her grow," Yvonne explained. "Tia is being selfish, and I'm hoping she'll consider other people and change her mind." She unfolded her arms and sat down in the black leather sofa.

"Mama, this is Tia's wedding, and she needs to feel comfortable when she walks down the aisle," Toya commented.

Thomas sat down on the sofa next to Yvonne. "Why do you think you'd be uncomfortable if your wedding was at Christ-Life?" he asked Tia.

"I don't want to walk down the aisle wondering if anyone is whispering about me. It's my day, and I'd like to enjoy it without unnecessary drama."

Yvonne wanted to tell Tia that she was responsible for most of the "unnecessary drama" in her life, but Thomas came to the rescue before she could open her mouth.

"If you're willing to get married as early as next month, I think I may have a solution to this problem."

"Next month is too soon," Tia said, shaking her head. "I don't think I could plan the wedding of my dreams in such a short time, Uncle Thomas."

"Girl, be quiet and let the man tell you what he has in mind before you say no," Toya advised her.

Yvonne looked over at Thomas. "What solution were you going to propose?"

"Well, I'm scheduled to preach in the Bahamas next month, and I was just thinking that the members of Christ-Life would not be offended if they weren't invited to a destination wedding. I would even pay for a honeymoon at the Atlantis on Paradise Island."

Tia's mouth hung open for a moment, and then she furrowed her brow. "Next month is July, Uncle Thomas. It's going to be too hot in the Bahamas."

"It may be hot," Thomas agreed, "but it will also be beautiful."

"Thomas, you shouldn't. This really is not your responsibility, and I can't have you dish out so much money for this wedding," Yvonne said.

"Trust me, Yvonne—it isn't a problem. And Tia is like a daughter to me. It would be my honor to cover the expenses."

Tia's mouth hung open for a moment. Then she turned and grabbed her purse, pulled out her cell phone, and punched in a number. Seconds later, she said, "Robbie, how would you like to get married in the Bahamas and honeymoon at the Atlantis in Paradise Island!" She paused, then added, "Uncle Thomas is going to pay for it." Her expression brightened as she listened to Robbie, and then she snapped the phone shut and beamed at Thomas. "We'll take it!"

Yvonne held up a hand. "Hold on, Tia. You told me you wanted to have eight bridesmaids and eight groomsmen. There's no way you can expect eight of your closest friends and eight of Robbie's to drop everything and fly to the Bahamas on such short notice."

Tia tapped her manicured nails on Yvonne's desk as she took a moment to think. "You might be right about that," she admitted. "But when you think about it, everybody I need is in this room. Toya can be my maid of honor, Uncle Thomas can walk me down the aisle, and you can marry us, Mama."

"Are you really willing to forgo the big wedding you've dreamed about since you were a little girl?" Yvonne asked her.

"Mom, I'm getting married in the Bahamas. What woman wouldn't want that? We won't have as many guests, but we can take plenty of pictures, and I'll share them with my friends. And if we have the wedding next month, I won't be showing that much—an added benefit of rushing this thing."

Yvonne gave Thomas's hand a squeeze. "I guess we're going to the Bahamas! Thanks, Thomas."

"Sure. I'll call a couple of churches down there and see which one will be available for the wedding."

"Ooh, can we have the wedding at Myles Munroe's church?" Toya asked.

"I don't know. We'll call and see what's on the agenda the week we'll be down there," Thomas said. He turned to Yvonne. "Can you have Dawn book several rooms for us at the Atlantis?"

"You give me the dates, and I'll have her get right on it."

"I'm going to need an extra room," Toya put in. "If I'm going to the Bahamas, I'm bringing a date."

Yvonne's eyes snapped to Toya. She had no clue that she was dating anyone. It was definitely time for her to get involved in her daughters' lives again. "I didn't know you were seeing anyone, Toya."

Toya nodded with a shy smile. "We've been dating for only about a month, but I really like him."

"Does he have a name?" Yvonne asked.

"This meeting is not about Toya's love life!" Tia put in. "I'm getting married in a month. Can we stay focused, people?"

"So sorry, Tia. We all know that this is your world, and we're just taking up space in it," Toya said. "What do you want us to do to help plan your wedding?"

Tia stood up from the desk, then grabbed Toya's hand and pulled her to her feet. "Let's go shopping. We don't have much time, so we are both getting something off the rack."

"You girls have fun. I'll see you when you get back," Yvonne said as they headed for the door.

Tia stopped and turned around. "You're not coming?" Her brown eyes looked sad, pleading.

"I wish I could, honey, but Thomas and I have a meeting with his accountant. I can't leave the office today, but you and I can get the plans moving this weekend, once we've secured a church for the ceremony."

Tia came over and gave her a kiss on the cheek. "Don't stress too much about finding a church, Mama. Shoot, I'm getting married in the Bahamas. We can do this thing on the beach, for all I care."

"Tia!" Yvonne exclaimed. After her daughter had told her that she was pregnant, Yvonne hadn't thought that Tia was capable of shocking her further. But getting married on the beach instead of in the house of God just didn't seem right. And it wasn't just because she was a preacher, either.

She was getting ready to tell Tia as much when Thomas put a hand on her arm. "Can you tell us why you would want to get married on a beach rather than inside of a church?" he asked Tia.

"It just seems so romantic." Tia twirled in a circle with a dreamy look in her eyes. She stopped and looked imploringly at Yvonne. "It's what I want, Mama, and I know that Robbie would agree. Can you please ask Dawn to see if we can do this wedding on the beach?"

No, and I'm not even going to take part in this pagan marry-because-I'm-knocked-up affair, Yvonne wanted to say. But because her love for Tia was greater than her indignation, she opened her mouth and said, "I'll have her check on it, sweetie."

"Thanks, Mama! You're the best. We'll see you later, okay?"

After Tia and Toya marched out of the office, looking anxious for a day of shopping, Yvonne fell back against the sofa, balled her fists, and stomped on the floor with the heel of her shoe a few times.

"Take a deep breath, Vonnie. This, too, shall pass," Thomas assured her.

No one had called her Vonnie for years. Brenda Reed had come up with the nickname, and David and Thomas had quickly picked it up when they were younger. "Oh, yeah? How can you be so sure?"

"My experience has made me believe the Bible when it says that *'our light affliction…is but for a moment.'*"

Yvonne sat up straighter and turned to face Thomas. "I don't know what I'm going to do. This Robbie guy that Tia is so excited to marry...he seems nice enough, but he's had five different jobs in the last two years. I'm worried that they won't be able to take care of themselves, let alone an innocent baby."

Thomas took Yvonne's hands in his. "There's no need for us to worry when we should be praying. Now, bow your head, and let's take this situation with Tia and hand it over to God."

Yvonne was glad to comply. She bowed her head and echoed in her heart what Thomas prayed aloud— at least for the first minute or so, until she started mulling over other matters.

She was grateful beyond words that Thomas had decided to stay and work at the church, despite her attempts to dissuade him. He had given the bank the money he'd promised in order to keep the church out of foreclosure, and now they were getting ready to meet with his accountant, who would go over the church books. Yvonne wanted to reassure Thomas that Christ-Life was a good investment and that he would get his money back.

"Amen," said Thomas to conclude the prayer.

Yvonne felt guilty for letting her mind wander while Thomas was praying, but she had so much on her mind that she found it impossible to focus on just one thing. "What time will the accountant be here, again?" she asked.

Thomas looked at his watch and stood up. "We should probably head to the conference room now. I'm sure he'll be here any minute."

Sure enough, there was a knock at the door. "Come in," Yvonne said as she got to her feet.

The door swung open, and Yvonne's assistant, Dawn, poked her head in. "There's a Mr. Samuel Johnson here to see you. He's in the conference room."

"Thank you, Dawn. Please tell him we'll be right there," Yvonne told her.

"Certainly, Pastor."

"Oh, and when Deacon Brown gets here, please send him to the conference room, as well," Yvonne added.

"Actually, Deacon Brown won't be coming," Dawn said. "He just called to say that he's got some type of flu bug, and that he won't be able to make the meeting."

"Well, if he's sick, he did the right thing by staying home," Yvonne replied. "I have way too much on my plate to get sick right now."

Dawn left, and Yvonne and Thomas made their way to the conference room, where a man in a checkered suit and a black bow tie was seated at the long table. He stood up when they entered. "Hello, Mr. Reed," he said, holding out his hand.

"Good to see you again, Sam," Thomas said. "This is Pastor Yvonne. Yvonne, Sam Johnson."

"Nice to meet you, Pastor," Sam said, nodding at Yvonne. He looked back at Thomas. "From what I hear, I guess I'm supposed to call you Pastor, too."

Thomas chuckled. "It's true that we'll be copastoring Christ-Life Sanctuary."

"For the time being," Yvonne put in.

Sam nodded and pushed his wire-rimmed glasses higher on his nose. "Well, shall we get started?"

The three of them sat down, and Sam pulled a file from his briefcase and set it on the table. "When will the finance director be here?" he asked.

"Deacon Brown is sick, so he won't be able to meet with us today," Thomas said.

"Some surprise that is," Sam said.

"Excuse me?" Yvonne raised her eyebrows at him. "Why would you say that?"

Sam pressed his palms to the table and leaned forward. "Let's just say that if I were a thief, I would be real sick right about now, too."

Chapter Seven

"To be honest with you, Mr. Johnson, I'm having a hard time understanding why you would come in here and malign a longtime member and deacon of this church," Yvonne said.

"I'm not trying to upset you, Pastor Yvonne, but the numbers don't lie," Sam replied.

Yvonne had known Deacon Clarence Brown for twenty years. And although the man had wanted to oust her from the pulpit, she still couldn't believe that he would steal money from the church. After all, it wasn't like robbing the church was a way to get back at her—anyone who robbed a church had to know he was robbing God, not the pastor.

Yvonne leaned over to reach the telephone on the conference room table and dialed Dawn's extension.

"Yes, Pastor Yvonne?" came Dawn's voice on the speakerphone.

"Dawn, can you get Deacon Brown on the phone, please?"

"Sure thing. I'll connect him to the conference room phone as soon as I reach him," Dawn said.

Yvonne looked at Thomas, then Sam. "We'll get to the bottom of this in just a few minutes."

"What leads you to believe that Deacon Brown has been stealing from the church?" Thomas asked Sam.

Sam cleared his throat and adjusted his glasses again as he sat up a bit straighter. "Well, first of all, I didn't receive the church financial records from Clarence Brown. As you know, after Thomas asked me to write that check to the bank, I wanted to see the files for the past five years, and your church administrator gave me access to them."

"That's right—Deacon Brown was on vacation," Yvonne confirmed, "and I asked our administrator to pull the files since I knew you needed the information in a hurry."

When the phone buzzed, Yvonne pressed the speakerphone button. "Did you get him?"

"No, I'm sorry, but Deacon Brown is not answering his home phone or his cell phone," Dawn informed her.

"Thanks. Just keep trying." That was odd. Deacon Brown rarely missed a meeting that had to do with the church's finances, and if he happened to be out of town or at home sick, he would call in and participate over the phone.

Yvonne turned back to Sam. "Okay, I'm all ears. What do you think is going on?"

Sam hesitated for a moment.

"Don't be shy, now," Thomas urged him. "Please, tell us what you found."

Sam folded his hands together and rested them on the table. "Well, my mother always said that the Lord works in mysterious ways, and we can be thankful for that. Because I can guarantee you that if Clarence Brown hadn't been on vacation when I asked for those files, I never would have been permitted to see these reports." Clearing his throat, he shuffled through a stack of papers and pulled out several that were marked with paperclips before continuing. "I reviewed the oldest financial statements first, and everything appeared to be in order for the first three years. Within the past two years, though, I don't know what happened, but your financial records became complete fiction."

"Are you referring to the fact that we are bringing in less money? If so, that can be explained." Yvonne was determined to defend Deacon Brown. She wanted to believe the best about him.

Sam held up a hand, then went on. "I am aware that your membership is down, and that a good portion of your members have been laid off. All of that information has been accounted for in the financial records. However, it is also clear to me that hundreds of thousands of dollars are missing—and not because of dwindling attendance and tithing."

"Exactly how much?" Thomas asked.

"About four hundred thousand—close to two hundred thousand each year for the past two years," Sam told them.

"Okay, so money is missing...probably an accounting error. Why are you so quick to assume that Deacon Brown did this deliberately?" Yvonne asked.

"The reports are so blatantly false that any accountant worth his CPA certificate would have found it. So, if Deacon Brown never mentioned this discrepancy to you, I can only assume that it's because he was responsible for it."

Yvonne wanted to disappear. If Deacon Brown had been robbing them for the past two years, as Sam was suggesting, then that meant that he had started right after David had been diagnosed with cancer. As she had spent more and more time with him at the hospital, Deacon Brown had continually assured her that she did not need to worry about the church—he would make sure all the bills were paid and keep the finances in order. All she needed to do was spend time with David. Yvonne had allowed him to handle everything, and she'd never questioned him, not even when he'd told her that they weren't bringing in enough money to meet their mortgage payments on the new building.

"The silver lining in all of this," Sam continued, "is that as long as you can eliminate whoever is responsible for stealing the money, your finances should stay afloat. You seem to be bringing in enough through tithes and offerings to pay your bills." He turned to Thomas and handed him a document. "I've come up with some projections to indicate how your three-hundred-thousand-dollar investment can be paid back."

Without looking at the paper, Thomas said, "We can discuss that at another time, Sam. Right now, I want to know what we can do to solve the immediate problem."

When the meeting with Samuel Johnson finally ended, Yvonne felt like three different kinds of fools. She had allowed her grief over David's illness and his subsequent death to take precedence over everything else, and now her younger daughter was pregnant and planning an after-the-fact wedding, her church falling apart, and one of her most trusted deacons was stealing money.

She plopped down on the sofa in her office, preparing to give herself a first-class pity party, when someone knocked on the door. She wanted to pretend that she wasn't there, just like her mother used to do when the insurance man would come to call. Yvonne's mother never seemed to have enough money to pay all of her bills, so she would just lock herself in the house and pretend that everything would turn out fine if she ignored reality. But then the electricity would be shut off. Their water would stop running.

Yvonne had promised herself that she would never run away from her responsibilities and just expect everything to turn out okay. But in the last eighteen months, she'd become more like her mother than ever before. It was time to step back into reality. "Come in," she said.

Thomas came in, and Yvonne wanted to get up and run to him. His presence exuded strength and confidence, and she needed those qualities right now. But she had already asked so much of Thomas that she didn't feel comfortable appointing him as her shoulder to cry on. So, she said a silent prayer, telling God that she was weak right now and asking Him to be her strength.

"I just showed Sam out, and I wanted to check on you," Thomas said, coming to sit next to her.

"You're a kind man, Thomas Reed."

"And you're a wonderful woman, Yvonne Milner." He grinned. "Okay, now that we've given each other praise and affirmation, we need to decide what we're going to do."

She turned away from him, ashamed about all that had happened while she had been busy grieving and not paying attention. She knew better than that. David had often quoted President Reagan's wisdom, "Trust, but verify." Why hadn't she bothered to double-check the church's financial records herself? But even as she asked herself the question, she knew the answer: It was because David had always reviewed the financial records. That wasn't her realm.

Yvonne turned to face Thomas. "I don't know what to do about anything, Thomas. I feel like every aspect of my life is falling apart. Tia's pregnant, Toya's dating someone I have never heard a word about—that makes me nervous—the church is falling apart, and now I find out that a man I have trusted for decades has been robbing the church blind. I haven't been handling my business well, so I really can't blame anyone but myself for what's going on."

"That's not true, Yvonne, and I'm not going to let you take the blame for Tia's actions," Thomas said sternly yet gently. "She is a grown woman, and you raised her to know right from wrong."

"But I haven't been there for her lately. I haven't been there for anyone. I've been too wrapped up in my own grief."

"Then, it was Tia's job to hold on to the truth in God that she had been taught all her life. She didn't, and she will have to deal with the consequences of her actions. All you can do is be there to hold her and assure her of your unconditional love."

Yvonne didn't respond. She just sat there with her hands in her lap.

"Toya's a big girl, too, and she has a good head on her shoulders, so you don't have to worry about her," Thomas continued. "And it is certainly not your fault that Deacon Brown turned out to be a thief. As for the church growth problem, my pledge to you is that Christ-Life Sanctuary will rise again. Because I'm not leaving until it does."

Yvonne gave a little half smile, but it quickly faded into a frown. "Oh, Thomas, I have been grossly unfair to you. I shouldn't have asked you to help me with the church; I should have resigned, just as I had decided to do at the board meeting."

Thomas held out his hand. "Follow me. I want to show you something."

"Where are we going?" she asked as she put her hand in his.

"Not far." He pulled her up from the sofa and walked her over to the window. Then, he pointed at the half finished Family Life Center. "Whose idea was that?"

Well, hers, of course. David had never wanted anything more than to preach Jesus and save souls. Yvonne had often asked him what they would do for the people after their souls had been saved, and David had always told her that Jesus would do the rest.

She believed that was true, and that spiritual growth could happen largely without the help of a church, through personal Bible study, prayer, and regular fellowship with God. But there were so many distractions, many of which hadn't been there thirty years ago when she and David had given their lives to the Lord. Yvonne believed that the people needed a Christian community—and a building to house it— where families could come and fellowship together without having to compromise their moral standards and religious beliefs. But Yvonne had been sidetracked by self-pity, and now that community was far from being a reality.

"It's not finished," she muttered. "It's been sitting there for an entire year, like an abandoned dream."

"It will be finished," Thomas said confidently. Then, he gently directed her away from the window. Still holding her hand, he opened her office door and led her down the hall to the sanctuary. They climbed up to the pulpit and looked out over the rows of pews. "Look at this incredible sanctuary," Thomas said. "David told me himself that he'd wanted to build a much smaller church, but you'd convinced him that if he did that, it would mean having to build again within the next few years. You are a visionary, Yvonne. God has you in the right place, and I don't ever want you to forget that. Okay?"

Yvonne looked up at Thomas. His face was set with determination, and those beautiful hazel eyes of his implored her to see things the way he saw them. A smile began to form on her face.

Before she could say anything, though, she and Thomas heard a commotion down the hall—voices shouting, it sounded like. They rushed down the steps in the sanctuary and into the hallway. When they rounded the corner to Dawn's office, they saw a group of people surrounding her desk. Yvonne counted ten women and six men. They were shouting angrily and holding pieces of paper in the air. "We've got to do something about this!" one of the men said.

A heavyset woman said, "Yeah! I know that Pastor Yvonne will never stand for it."

As she and Thomas approached the group, Yvonne recognized some of them as people who lived in the neighborhood nearby and also attended the church. At least, they had attended the church at one point in time if they no longer did. Yvonne hadn't seen some of these people in months. "What's going on?" she asked them.

One woman broke away from the pack and turned toward her. Yvonne recognized her as Marley Parker, a seventy-year-old widow who lived in a house across the street from the church. "Pastor Yvonne!" she said in a quaking voice. "They're trying to take our homes." She thrust a folded letter into Yvonne's hands.

"Who is trying to take your homes?" Thomas asked, a look of confusion on his face.

"The government," said an elderly man with a cane. He hobbled closer and handed Thomas his letter.

Yvonne began reading and saw that the city government had indeed offered to pay a fair price for each person's home. Perhaps "offered" was too generous a term. These letters were basically demands that the residents vacate their properties based on eminent domain.

Something else in the letter stood out to her: it stated that every home or structure within a five-mile radius would be purchased and that the area would be rezoned as a business district.

Yvonne turned to Dawn. "Did we receive a letter like this?"

"Yes, we did. I had just started going through the mail when everyone came in." Dawn held up a piece of paper and handed it to Yvonne. It looked identical to the one Mrs. Parker had given her.

Thomas reached out his hand. "Let me see that."

Yvonne handed him the letter. She didn't need to read it. She knew it would say the same thing that all the other letters did.

Would her problems never end? First, the church board had tried to take the church from her, and now the government wanted her church and all the houses that surrounded it. Thomas had just spent several minutes trying to revive the visionary in her, and she was thankful for that, because she envisioned a fight in her future.

Chapter Eight

AFTER THE GROUP HAD DISPERSED, WITH THOMAS AS-suring them that something would be done to protect their homes, Yvonne went back to her office, closed the door, and got down on her knees to pray. When she finally got up off the floor, she sat down at her desk and began to formulate a plan of action. Most of the people who'd come to the church for help today no longer attended Christ-Life. A few of them had admitted that they had joined a different church, but more of them had said they had stopped attending church altogether. That knowledge got Yvonne to thinking.

She picked up the phone and dialed Elder Dwight Conrad. Besides being on the church board, Elder Conrad headed up the evangelistic team, a group that organized outreaches to communicate the good news of Jesus Christ. If there was anyone who could accomplish what Yvonne needed to have done right now, it was the evangelistic team.

After two rings, Elder Conrad picked up. "Hello, Elder Conrad. It's Pastor Yvonne. I know you're busy, so I'm not going to keep you long, but I do need your help."

"Name it, Pastor. Whatever I can do, I'd be honored to help you."

"First of all, is your team in the middle of a particular outreach right now?"

"As a matter of fact, we just finished a door-to-door campaign in a local neighborhood, and we're meeting next Friday to plan our next mission."

"Do you have the specifics of that project planned out already?"

"To tell you the truth, Pastor, I have been trying to come up with an idea for about a month now, but every time I think of something, I feel like God is telling me, 'That's not it.' I've been getting nervous. I have no idea what I'm going to present to my team," Elder Conrad confessed.

Yvonne had to smile. God was being good to her, even though she neither knew nor understood what He was doing. She was certain that Elder Conrad's "lack of inspiration" had been on purpose because God was waiting on Yvonne to wake up and do something about a problem. "If you don't mind, Elder Conrad, I have a project that your team could help me with."

"What would you like us to do?"

"I would appreciate it if your team would check in on the members of Christ-Life who have recently left the church."

"All right, Pastor; that sounds fine. But how will we know who to talk to?"

"I'll have Dawn check our attendance records and generate a list of people who haven't attended in the past six months. After I send you the list, I would like for your team to contact each individual or family, whether by calling them, e-mailing them, or knocking on their door."

"Is there something specific you'd like us to say to them?" Elder Conrad asked.

"Yes, I think there is. First, ask how he or she or the family is doing. Then, ask if they've joined a new church. Finally, see whether they need prayer or any other type of assistance from us. Things like that."

"Sounds good. We can do that," Elder Conrad assured her. "How soon do you think you could have the list to me?"

"I'll have to check with Dawn, but I'm sure she will be able to send it before you meet with the group next Friday."

"Okay, Pastor. Consider it done."

"Elder Conrad, one more thing," Yvonne said, hoping to catch him before he hung up. "If some of the people you talk to have joined a new church, I don't want anyone pressuring them to come back to Christ-Life. Just bless them and pray with them if they need it."

"And what if they haven't joined a new church and are just sitting at home with no desire to go to services?"

Yvonne smiled to herself. "Those are the people I'm really interested in. Tell them that things are moving forward at Christ-Life. Tell them that Pastor Yvonne sends her apologies for not being the leader they needed her to be, and that—"

"With all due respect, Pastor, I don't think you owe anyone an apology for grieving the loss of your husband. And if you want my opinion, it's the people who left while we were in transition who should be apologizing to you."

Yvonne was silent as she considered his comment.

"And I owe you an apology, too," Elder Conrad continued. "I didn't stand up for you like I should have at our last board meeting. I let other people sway me, and I'm sorry for that. It will never happen again."

Although she considered Elder Conrad's apology unnecessary, Yvonne was still grateful for it. "Thank you, Elder Conrad. Well then, if we're not going to be giving the people my apologies, please just tell them that the highly esteemed Thomas Reed has joined our ministry as copastor, and that we'd like to know what it would take to get them to come back home."

They talked about the new evangelistic campaign for a few minutes before saying their good-byes. When she hung up the phone, Yvonne felt energized. She had only just begun to fight. She wanted to call the police regarding Deacon Brown and turn over all of the evidence that Sam had given them so that the man would rot in prison for the rest of his days. But she didn't have time to deal with that right now. The money was gone, and she doubted they would get it back. Right now, she needed to concentrate on this business about the government trying to take away her church and the homes surrounding it.

Every way I turn, someone's trying to crucify me, she thought. *Well, I'm not getting on that cross without a fight.* She picked up the phone and called her long-time friend, Serenity Williams. Actually, her name was Serenity McKnight now. Serenity had married Pastor Phillip McKnight, a retired NFL football player, after a whirlwind courtship of six months. The McKnights lived in Tampa, and Serenity had moved her Christian television talk show down there from Chicago. Yvonne had met Serenity at a women's conference and had appeared as a guest on her show countless times. Over the years, Serenity and Yvonne, along with Melinda Marks, a pastor in Baltimore, had become close, Yvonne acting as a big sister and spiritual mentor for the two younger women. After David had died, however, Yvonne had shied away from both of them, even though they'd called often to see how she was doing and if she needed anything. Not wanting to rain on their parades of marital love, Yvonne had kept the conversations short and had recently stopped returning their calls.

Even though the site where Serenity filmed her show had changed, it was still nationally syndicated, and Yvonne knew that a story about the government trying to take over a community and the church that was its cornerstone would be of interest to her friend and her viewers.

"Well, hello, stranger!" Serenity answered on the first ring.

"Hey, Serenity!" said Yvonne. "I'm sorry that I've been out of reach these past few months. But I'm back now, and I could use your help with something."

"What's up?" Serenity asked.

"Before I bore you with the details of my crucifixion saga, please tell me how you and Phillip are doing."

"Oh, we're doing great—Phillip is still the most wonderful man I know. I could kick myself for almost letting him get away. Now, what's this about a crucifixion saga? Who's trying to crucify you?"

"Who isn't?" Yvonne said, shaking her head. "But what I need your help with is fighting off the government."

"Good thing you don't ask for much," Serenity said with a laugh.

"Girl, this is going to be a big favor, so I'll understand if you can't help. But if you can, I would greatly appreciate it."

"Start from the top. Tell me what's going on and what you want me to do about it."

Yvonne took a deep breath and began. She told Serenity that the city government had declared its intention to seize her church and the homes surrounding it, according to eminent domain, and that the plan was to purchase their property and tear down everything they'd spent years building to develop a business district.

"You're kidding!" Serenity said when Yvonne had concluded her narrative.

"I wish I was."

"Okay, well, what do you need me to do?" Serenity sounded like she was ready to go to war with Yvonne.

"I was hoping that you might have time to do a segment on our situation here in Detroit."

"I like it. I will fly up there early next week so we can tape the show and have it on the air as soon as possible."

"Oh, Serenity, thank you! I can't tell you how much this means to me."

"And you don't have to. See you next week."

After they'd ended the conversation and hung up, Yvonne leaned back in her leather chair, propped her feet on the foot rest, and closed her eyes. She needed a moment of nothingness so she could collect her thoughts. Her experiences in the past several weeks had drained her, left her weak. She was thinking about rejuvenation as she drifted off to sleep. But the Spirit of the Lord must have had other things in store for her, for the dream that filled her mind had little to do with rejuvenation. It took her back to a time before she was even a thought in her mama's mind. As a matter of fact, back then, nobody had been thinking about her mama, her mama's mama, and so on.

Yvonne stood on the side of a rough and dusty road as she watched a man carry this big, wooden cross.

The crowd around her seemed electrified by the scene. But Yvonne was bothered by what was happening, even though she didn't know this man. Meanwhile, the crowd grew more and more excited, and she saw several men actually spit on the helpless man carrying the cross. He fell down, and it appeared as if he could go no further. He couldn't carry that heavy cross all by himself anymore. Several men in uniform—guards, so it seemed—began to beat the poor, defenseless man. Yvonne wanted to run to him, pick up the cross, and carry it for him herself. But before she could move, another man with compassion in his eyes knelt down beside the man, lifted the cross from his shoulders, and began to carry it.

When he reached his destination, the man received no rest. A crown of thorns was placed on his head, and blood began to trickle from his head down his face. He did not resist when the soldiers roughly thrust him against the cross, and he did not protest as another soldier drove a nail through his left hand. The nail was thick, like a spike, and Yvonne could not imagine the pain he must be feeling. When his right hand was nailed to the cross, Yvonne screamed, but it seemed as though no one had heard her.

By now, she had figured out just who was being nailed to that cross. And as the cross was raised between two crosses where two other men were being crucified, even though she had never studied Latin, she knew that the sign atop the middle cross read, "This is Jesus, the King of the Jews." Her precious Savior was on that cross, right before her very eyes. He had been beaten, spit on, and brutally nailed to a cross, and now He watched as men divided up the very clothes that had been on His back.

Jesus looked to heaven with tears in His eyes and said, "Father, forgive them, for they know not what they do."

Yvonne jolted awake and realized she was shaking uncontrollably. She began to calm down, but her heart almost stopped at a sudden realization. She had told Serenity that she was being crucified, but with the raw images of Jesus' death in her mind, she realized she had no right to compare what was happening to her to a crucifixion. Yes, it was true that she had been wronged, but she was no one's savior. She didn't have to come back to heal and help the very people who were trying to do her in, albeit in a figurative sense. As a matter of fact, she hadn't even been thinking about turning the other cheek. She had wanted to get them—some of the board members, Deacon Brown, the government—the way they had gotten her. But as she recalled her Savior's response to the men who were wronging Him to the point of death, she knew she had some serious repenting to do.

She had just witnessed a vision of her Savior being mistreated in the most ungodly fashion imaginable. He could have summoned a legion of angels to fight His battle, and yet He had chosen to have mercy on the offenders. "Father, forgive me. What was I thinking?" she prayed fervently. "Vengeance is Yours, not mine. Help me through all of this madness, and I promise that I will never repay evil with evil."

Chapter Nine

$\mathcal{T}$RUE TO HER WORD, SERENITY CAME TO DETROIT WITH her film crew the following week. The cameramen walked around the church, taking pictures of the sanctuary, the fellowship hall, and the half finished Family Life Center. The crew also got footage of some of the homes in the nearby neighborhoods. Then, Serenity, Yvonne, and Thomas sat down to talk. Of course, their conversation was conducted beneath bright lights and in front of cameras and microphones.

Serenity was the picture of professionalism in her hunter green linen pantsuit and two-tone Italian leather pumps. Yvonne smiled, knowing full well that although Serenity's attire made it look as if her husband was still receiving an NFL salary, her friend had probably purchased each item at a secondhand shop. The girl loved her bargain boutiques. Yvonne wished she could put herself together as well as Serenity and still leave some money in the bank.

"Welcome to *Walk This Way!*" Serenity began, smiling at the camera. "I have a special treat for my audience today, because I am sitting with two of the most dynamic personalities in Christendom today: Pastor Yvonne Milner, of Christ-Life Sanctuary in Detroit, and the world-renowned speaker and teacher, Thomas Reed."

Serenity turned toward Thomas and Yvonne as the camera crew moved in for a closer shot. "Pastor Yvonne, it is so good to have you on the program again. I know you've gone through some difficult changes since the last time you were our guest. Would you care to tell our audience a little bit about that?"

Yvonne really didn't want to share any intimate details with strangers, but she'd asked for this interview, and she trusted Serenity. So, she stepped out in faith to answer the question. "Yes, there have been some changes since the last time we spoke on your show. The most significant change is that my husband of over thirty years passed away."

Serenity's expression turned deeply compassionate. "That was a sad time for the body of Christ. I know that my husband and I prayed that Pastor David would survive, but we all know that to be absent from the body is to be present with the Lord. So, he is in a much better place."

"Thank you for saying that, Serenity." Yvonne smiled. "I know that David is home with the Lord, and that brings me comfort."

Serenity turned to Thomas. "From what I hear, I need to call you 'Pastor Reed' again. Am I right?"

"That's right. I'm getting too old to travel all over the world," Thomas joked. "I needed a place to settle these old bones."

"You are far from old, Pastor Reed, but what you are doing here is quite momentous. Not many people would give up their successful careers to help a friend in need."

Yvonne leaned over and gave Thomas's hand a grateful squeeze. "But Thomas is more than a friend—he's family," she put in. "I am so thankful that he decided to come and help me, but it's only temporary. Thomas will be back on the road fulfilling his ministry assignments just as soon as he is ready to go."

Serenity clasped her hands. "Okay, Pastor Yvonne. I'm sure other pastors are wondering why you would need help with your church. After all, you've been pastoring for more than twenty years."

Yvonne wanted to send a signal to Serenity to tell her she wanted to answer questions only if they dealt with the problem she was having with the City of Detroit trying to take her church away. She didn't want to tell the world that she was incompetent and couldn't handle the responsibilities of pastoring a church on her own.

Thankfully, Thomas chimed in. "It's simple, really. After David died, the recession hit. Christ-Life Sanctuary lost a lot of members, and the financing dried up because many of the remaining members had lost their jobs in the auto industry. So, I answered God's call to step in and help Yvonne and Christ-Life Sanctuary through this transitional time."

"After you came on board, things seemed to be turning around," Serenity said. "But now, you've just been hit with some news—bad news for the church, and bad news for the community that surrounds the church." She shifted her gaze to Yvonne. "Pastor Yvonne, can you tell us about this new threat that is attempting to tear down the church you and your husband founded over two decades ago?"

Yvonne smiled. Finally, she was in the territory she wanted to be in. Although she understood Serenity's technique in building up to this moment, the implication that she could not handle the church on her own still hurt. But she was in her element now, ready to fight for justice for Christ-Life Sanctuary and for the people in the surrounding community.

She turned to Serenity and recounted everything they knew about the city's plans to demolish the church and the nearby homes in order to turn the area into a business district. When Yvonne had finished, Serenity asked Thomas to give the closing prayer.

Once the cameras were turned off, Serenity said, "I'm sorry if I made you feel a little uncomfortable with some of my questions, Yvonne. But viewers love a human interest story, so we have to give them enough to grab hold of. Okay?"

Yvonne leaned over and gave Serenity a hug. "It's more than okay. I appreciate what you just did for me. I just hope it makes a difference."

"Hey, none of that hoping stuff," came a voice from offstage. "You taught me to have faith and believe that certain things will come to pass."

Yvonne recognized the voice and couldn't believe what she was hearing. She turned around to see Melinda Marks standing there with her hands on her hips. Yvonne jumped out of her chair to greet Melinda but stopped to look back at Serenity, who was smiling mischievously. "You didn't tell me that Melinda was coming!" she said in a scolding tone.

"She wanted to surprise you," Serenity said.

Yvonne turned back to Melinda and rushed over to give her a hug, but Melinda's belly was in the way. "Girl, how many kids are you and Steven going to have? Pretty soon, the two of you will have your own reality show, competing with Michelle Duggar for the 'Most Kids by One Mother' award."

"That's not fair, Yvonne," Melinda defended herself. "This is only my third pregnancy."

"Yeah, but you've been married for only three and a half years," Serenity pointed out in a teasing voice.

"You leave me alone, too, Serenity. I can't help it if my man is virile. You and Phillip need to start working on your own family, anyway," Melinda told her.

Serenity stalked over to her. "Who's to say that we haven't already started working on our own family?"

The room went silent for a moment. Melinda looked Serenity up and down. "Are you trying to tell us something?"

"Whatever would I have to tell you? All I did was take a home pregnancy test," Serenity said calmly, then added with elevated excitement, "that came out positive!"

"What fantastic news!" Yvonne exclaimed as she joined in a group hug with Melinda and Serenity. "This calls for a celebration." She wanted to tell them that Tia was pregnant, too, but she didn't know if Tia would want her to share the news, especially since she wasn't married yet. For a moment, Yvonne realized how awful it was to expect a grandchild and not be able to celebrate.

Yvonne was in the mood for King Louie crab legs again, so she took Serenity and Melinda to lunch at Bourbon Steak. As they sat and reminisced about memorable moments and discussed how the position of women in ministry had changed over the years, Yvonne found herself beginning to relax. She was among friends, so she could let her hair down and confess her thoughts and fears. "When all of my problems with the church started, I kept thinking that if I lost my church, I would set the cause of women in ministry back a decade," she admitted.

"Why would you think that?" Serenity asked.

"Because I have been so vocal about women in ministry. I speak about it all the time—that women are just as capable as men to lead a ministry. And now, here I am, having to lean on Thomas Reed to help me fix what I've messed up."

"I think you're being too hard on yourself," Melinda said. "We all know how hard it was on you to lose David. Anybody would have had a tough time coming back after what you went through and running this mammoth-sized ministry you and Pastor David started together."

"I appreciate your saying that, but I know I messed up," Yvonne said. "I allowed my grief to stop me from doing my job effectively, and the ministry suffered. It's one of the reasons some men say women should never be in positions of leadership in churches—because we're too emotional."

"But you don't believe that," Serenity reminded her. She was now copastor of New Destiny Church, where her husband, Phillip, was the senior pastor. Initially wary of getting involved in church ministry, Serenity had matured in her faith, discerned and accepted God's will, and grown comfortable in her leadership role.

Yvonne looked at Serenity, then at Melinda. She knew that these young women looked to her for wisdom. They were her daughters in Christ, and she would not let them down. "No, Serenity, I don't believe that. I think a healthy dose of emotion helps us to be a little more compassionate concerning the things that trouble the people we serve. I was just making an observation about how my failure would look to some people."

"Well, you don't have to worry about that now," Melinda said, "because you are *not* going to fail."

"That's right," Serenity agreed. "You will succeed, and your ministry will thrive again, especially now that you've got that fine copastor working with you," she added with a sly smile.

Yvonne dropped her jaw and let her mouth hang open for a moment before responding. "Serenity Mc-Knight, you are a married woman!"

"Hey, I might be married, but that doesn't mean that I've lost my sight," Serenity said with a giggle. "But even if I couldn't see, I would know that Thomas Reed was something special. The man exudes confidence. He's got charm and charisma like nothing I've ever seen. Phillip was a bit awkward around me at first, and I can't imagine Thomas being awkward around any woman."

"Serenity has a point there," Melinda admitted. "I thank God that Steven has never been too dashing or debonair. But I wouldn't have been upset if he'd taken a few lessons in smoothness from Pastor Reed. The man just owns any room he happens to be in."

Yvonne rolled her eyes. "You two need to quit! Thomas isn't Mr. Smoothness, Mr. Charisma, or anything else. He's simply a good friend who wants to help—that's it, and that's all."

"If you say so," Serenity said. "But I'll tell you what. Men like Thomas Reed don't stay single for long. Some woman is going to snatch him up...and I'm thinking that it might as well be you, Yvonne. I mean, the two of you are already running a ministry together."

Yvonne shook her head in disbelief. "David and I were married for over thirty years, and I loved him with all my heart. I can't see loving anyone else like that. So, I'd rather be single the rest of my life than make another man deal with the ghost of my husband."

"I know that the loss of a spouse is one of the hardest things to get over," Melinda said. "My dad took a long time to get over my mother's death. That's why he didn't remarry for so many years. But he's in his eighties now, and he and Barbara have been married for two years. And he's completely in love with her."

"See, Yvonne? Anything's possible," Serenity chimed in.

Yvonne laughed. "I can guarantee you that I won't be walking down the aisle anytime soon. Nor anytime later. I married the love of my life, and now that he's in heaven, I will live out my life with his memory. That will be enough for me."

Chapter Ten

SERENITY HAD BEEN RIGHT ABOUT THE MEDIA AND viewers grabbing hold of the human interest side of the story. Serenity's segment on Christ-Life had aired last Monday, and ever since then, Thomas and Yvonne had been bombarded with interviews from local and national news stations. It seemed that everyone wanted to know more about the partnership that Thomas and Yvonne had forged, as well as the issue of Christ-Life being sold to the city and then bulldozed. CNN and MSNBC even picked up the story. By Friday, someone from the Detroit mayor's office had called and invited them to a meeting on Monday.

That's why Thomas was driving around town with his digital camera, scouting out locations that the city could use for land development. It was probably their one and only chance to convince the mayor to build his new business district elsewhere. Thomas planned to go to the meeting armed with so much ammunition that the mayor wouldn't be able to do anything but change his mind—that, or wind up on CNN, looking like the mayor who stole a church.

There were so many empty storefronts and closed businesses in Detroit that it was impossible to go a mile without seeing a "Closed" or "For Sale" sign. It struck Thomas as odd that the city would choose to tear down an entire community where the people had lived most of their lives in order to develop a new business district when there were so many other areas in the city that could be used. As a matter of fact, the city wouldn't have to spend so much money purchasing buildings only to tear them down if they used some of the wasteland that Thomas had found and photographed—acres and acres of land with nothing on it. So, why, again, would a city that was in desperate need of funds choose to spend so much money to buy property that had already been developed with a church and private residences, only to tear them down and start over, when there was land aplenty that wasn't being used for anything?

Thomas didn't have answers to those questions, but he intended to get some. He planned to give the mayor an earful—and an eyeful.

Thomas was so pumped about the meeting that he didn't even care about the sleep he was missing. He had preached the sermon at church the day before. Normally, whenever he spoke somewhere, he would spend the following morning at home or in his hotel room, resting. Preaching wore him out, and he always wanted to deliver his best to the people of God. That is why he also studied God's Word on a regular basis and planned his sermons or motivational speeches well in advance. He reviewed his recordings of prior messages and watched films of himself, listening to the way he spoke to the crowd, always with an eye and an ear for improving. He had become one of the most highly sought-after speakers because of his natural yet poetic prose when he spoke to an audience. He tried to embody a blend of the styles of Dr. Martin Luther King Jr. and Les Brown.

So, even though he wanted to rest today, Thomas couldn't have afforded to stay in bed one extra minute. He was on a mission, and nothing was going to get in his way. Not even his publisher, who was calling him on his cell phone this very moment. Thomas put down his camera to answer the phone. "Hey, Fred. If you're calling, I know I must be in big trouble," he joked.

Although he had gone out to dinner a few times with Fred Tompkins, the head of the company that published his books, he normally spoke only with his editor, Maryann. If she had called on the big guns for help, there must be a serious problem related to his latest manuscript.

"No trouble at all, Thomas. I was just talking with Maryann, and she doesn't think that your book will go to press on time if your manuscript isn't in by the end of this week."

No trouble, huh? "Fred, I'm not trying to be difficult, but I'm going to need more time. I have delivered ten other books ahead of schedule, but right now, I have other priorities that I can't ignore."

"How much of the book have you completed?"

"About half."

"And how much more time do you think you'll need to get the rest of it done?"

Thomas made a mental checklist of all of the things he had to deal with: Deacon Brown's theft, the property seizure issue, and Tia's destination wedding. He didn't know how long it would take him to get those items wrapped up, so he really couldn't commit to a specific date. Hesitantly, he replied, "I really couldn't say."

"If memory serves me right, you normally dictate your books into a recording device before you write them down."

"Yeah, and I've already done that; I just don't have time to type it out and polish it up." Thomas's recordings were the unrefined "raw materials" of his books, and sometimes putting his thoughts and teachings into a style appropriate for the printed page took longer than it did to come up with them in the first place.

"Well, why don't you send those tapes to us?" Fred suggested. "Maryann can have someone type everything up, and then she'll polish it, as you normally would. Then, we'll e-mail the manuscript back to you so that you can look it over and make changes as needed."

Thomas took a deep breath as he considered Fred's idea. "That would help me out, Fred," he finally said. "I really appreciate that you're willing to do this for me."

"Hey, we're partners in this, remember? We understand that you've taken on new responsibilities at Christ-Life Sanctuary, and we want you to know that we're here to help in whatever way we can."

"Well, again, I just hope you realize how much I appreciate your support."

"Don't worry about it," Fred said. "And tell Pastor Yvonne that we are anxiously awaiting her next book, so she can just let us know when she has another one in the works."

"I'll do that," Thomas said. "Thanks again, Fred."

He was grateful that his book project could move forward without his full participation, because nothing could get him off course right now. He was determined to make things right for Yvonne, even if he had to spend every waking moment trying to get to the bottom of what exactly was going on with the city of Detroit and its property seizure plans.

He was also glad to hear that Fred wanted another book from Yvonne. That news would surely perk up her spirits. He had been partly responsible for Yvonne's first book deal with that publishing house. At the Independent Christian Retail Show almost two decades ago, she and David had insisted he introduce Yvonne to his publisher. *"Yvonne has a book that every woman in this country needs to read,"* David had told him. *"You've got to help her out, Thomas."*

At those words, Thomas had almost laughed in his friend's face. For years, David had been a hard sell on women preachers, and it wasn't until Thomas had preached a message at Christ-Life Sanctuary about the call of God on women in ministry that David's mind and heart had begun to change. Thomas had been a little apprehensive about preaching that message. At the time, he was pastoring a floundering church and really needed the extra income the speaking engagement would bring. So, he hadn't wanted to offend his friend. But Thomas never played around when the Lord gave him a message to deliver, so he had gone ahead and preached it with conviction.

"You can get that smirk off your face, Thomas Reed," David had said. "You started all of this. If you hadn't opened my eyes to the reality that women can and should be preachers, I wouldn't be working to further my wife's ambitions. But I'm telling you, Yvonne's name is going to be bigger than mine one day."

"Okay, okay," Thomas had said with a chuckle. "Follow me. I'll introduce you and Yvonne to my publisher, Fred Tompkins."

And that's where it had all started. Yvonne's first book was titled *Girl, Free Yourself.* It encouraged women to reclaim the power that God had given them through the death, burial, and resurrection of Jesus Christ, and it had become a number one best seller. The book was still popular and continued to sell well in bookstores and online. *That's what Yvonne needs*, Thomas thought to himself as he continued to drive down the street, scouting out potential locations for the city's new business district. *A new book to write.*

In his office, Marvel Williams sat with his feet propped up on his desk and paged through a copy of *Girl, Free Yourself.* He despised the author of that book for more reasons than he could count. And he had finally devised a plan to pay her back for everything she had taken from him.

Yes, Mrs. Say-It-like-It-Is Yvonne Milner had taken a lot from him, including both his parents. After reading the pages of hogwash in *Girl, Free Yourself,* his weak-minded mother had somehow gained a sense of empowerment and left his father. And then his father had politely put a bullet in his mother's head for having the audacity to think that she could do better than him.

Marvel had been placed in foster care, where he had remained until he turned eighteen and left for college on a scholarship. So, the way Marvel saw it, since Yvonne had taken his mother and his father from him, he was going to take her daughter from her. He had had no home after his father was arrested, so he was going to make sure that Yvonne lost her church home.

For a while, everything was falling into place, but then that weasel Thomas Reed came riding in to save the day, Clarence Brown got cold feet and skipped town on him, and then Pastor Yvonne and Thomas started telling their sob story on every radio station and television show they could find. Marvel hadn't been worried until CNN had covered the story. After that, his contact in the mayor's office also started to get cold feet.

Things might not be going according to plan, but with his high IQ and his ability to convince others to believe anything he wanted them to, Marvel was sure he would get the job done. He just had to keep Toya in the dark about what he was doing with her mother's church long enough to get what he wanted from her—the piece of this entire plan that would rip Yvonne Milner's heart out. Marvel planned to marry Toya and then make her life a living hell, just as his father had done to his mother. Then maybe he'd give her a copy of *Girl, Free Yourself,* so he could go and spend some quality time with his father in prison.

To make his plan work, he also had to keep Toya from learning about his business dealings. Toya had it in her mind to go to the meeting with the mayor tonight to support her mother, but that was the last place Marvel wanted her to be. Some fool would probably let it slip that he was the businessman who had requested the right to build his factory right where Christ-Life Sanctuary currently sat. He didn't think Toya would take that information too well, so he picked up the phone and dialed her number. When Toya answered, Marvel said, "Hey, baby! How's your day going?"

"It was pretty hectic until I received those flowers from you. I couldn't believe you remembered that we met two months ago today!"

"How could I forget? You've made my time in Detroit very pleasant."

"Why, thank you, sir," she said with a giggle.

"Hey, I was calling to see if you'd like to have dinner with me tonight to celebrate our anniversary."

"Oh, I'd love to, but I have to go to that meeting with my mom—remember, the one I told you about with the mayor?"

He snapped his fingers. "That's right. I forgot about that." He paused for a moment. "How about you let me take you out for an early dinner, and then I'll drop you off at the meeting? That way, you can celebrate with me and still be there for your mom."

"Ah, you're so sweet! Okay, pick me up at work around five thirty, and we'll go celebrate."

Marvel really liked Toya. If her mother were not the evil preacher who'd caused his mother's death, he thought that he and Toya could have made things work. Too bad he had to destroy her. But, hey, an eye for an eye; a daughter for a mother. "I can't wait to see you."

"Hey, Marvel? Are you still on for coming to the Bahamas for my sister's wedding?"

"Of course. Why wouldn't I want to go to the Bahamas with you?"

"Well, because we'll be in separate rooms."

"That's the thing I don't get. If you're into me enough to ask me to go to the Bahamas with you, why can't we stay in the same room?" Marvel asked. He thrilled to think of Pastor Yvonne having a stroke after discovering that he had slept with her perfect daughter.

"I've explained this to you before, Marvel. I know that I am twenty-six years old, but the only man I intend to sleep with is my husband. It's the way I was raised, and I plan to honor my vows to God," Toya told him with conviction in her voice.

"I can understand that, Toya. I've made a few vows to God, as well. And believe me, I plan to honor every one of them."

"Have you found a church home yet?" Toya wanted to know.

Marvel sighed. "Not yet. I've been visiting different churches, but none of them has felt like home."

"Why don't you come to church with me on Sunday? I guarantee that you will love my mother's church."

"I've told you before, Toya, I don't want to attend church with you until we determine where our relationship is heading. It would be different if your mother wasn't the pastor. But since she is, the whole idea is kind of uncomfortable for me." *In more ways than one.*

"All right, Marvel. But you don't want to bounce around from one church to the next for too long. It's always good to have a church family, even if it isn't 'perfect'—because you know that no perfect church exists."

"Don't you worry about me, little Miss Toya. I don't intend to bounce around for much longer. Soon, I'll find what I've been looking for, and then everything else will fall into place."

Chapter Eleven

*Y*VONNE WAS LOSING PATIENCE. SHE AND THOMAS WERE waiting for the mayor to grace them with his presence. They had accommodated his busy schedule by agreeing to meet with him at his office at seven in the evening, but it was already twenty-five after seven, and still the mayor hadn't shown up. She was beginning to think that he had forgotten about them.

"Can you believe this man is making us wait like this?" Thomas asked, voicing the same feeling of being slighted that Yvonne was experiencing.

She looked down at her watch. "Toya was supposed to meet us here, too. I don't know what's keeping her." She pulled out her phone and was preparing to call her daughter when the door to the mayor's office opened. She put the cell phone back in her purse.

The man introduced himself as Michael Barclay, an official in the mayor's office. "Sorry I'm late," he said as he took a seat behind the mayor's desk. "It's been a madhouse around here today."

"I'm glad you showed up. I was beginning to wonder," Thomas said as he glanced at his watch. "How much longer will we have to wait for the mayor to get here?"

"I'm sorry if the mayor's executive assistant didn't explain this meeting correctly," Michael explained.

"The mayor is out of town, and your meeting was scheduled with me."

"And who exactly are you?" Thomas asked testily.

Yvonne put a gentle hand on Thomas's shoulder. She recognized that he was about to go tickety-boom, and she wanted to quiet things down before the bomb exploded. "Mr. Barclay, we thought our meeting was with the mayor," she said calmly. "Is there some reason that he sent you, instead?"

"Yes, of course there is," Michael said loftily. "I am the person handling the eminent domain seizure of property in the neighborhood where your church building is located, and so the mayor knew I would have the information you are looking for."

"Okay! Now we're getting somewhere," Yvonne said, releasing Thomas's shoulder. "I do have a few questions for you, Mr. Barclay. First, I'd like to know why our area was picked for this business district you want to develop."

"There were several considerations that went into selecting the location for the new factory that will be constructed," Michael explained, "but the most important factor had to do with the priorities and preferences of the factory owner."

"And just who might that be?" Thomas asked, his tone slightly less irritated but far from placid.

"I'm not at liberty to divulge that information at this time. But I can tell you that this factory is slated to bring about five hundred jobs to the city—jobs we desperately need."

"I understand the need for jobs, but the people in our church community have lived in their homes for years," Yvonne explained. "They've raised their children in those homes, and now their grandchildren visit them there. They don't want to uproot and move somewhere else just to make room for a factory."

"It's not as if we're just taking the houses without paying for them," Michael responded. "Believe me, everyone in that neighborhood will have more than enough money to purchase another house."

"Money isn't everything, Mr. Barclay. You're trying to take homes away from people based simply on the whim of someone who might decide to move his factory somewhere else."

"We don't believe that will happen. And remember, Pastor Yvonne, we are willing to pay two million dollars for your church. I'm sure you can relocate easily with that kind of money."

"We owe three million on that building. How in the world could the government offer me less than what I owe and consider that fair?" Yvonne's voice rose in pitch, and she found herself unable to quiet it.

"You have a structure on your land that is not finished. That is why the property has been devalued." Michael shrugged. "I'm sorry, but unless you can get that structure finished quickly, we can't pay you any more than the standing offer."

Yvonne was speechless. The government wanted to throw her out of her church and leave her with a million-dollar debt?

"Why don't you just provide this person with another location for his factory?" Thomas asked.

Michael turned to him and said, "This was the best location available for our buyer's needs."

"Oh, really?" With that, Thomas leaned over, opened his briefcase, and pulled out a file folder. He set the folder on the desk and produced one picture after the next of abandoned buildings or empty lots. "Were any of these locations considered?"

Now it was Michael's turn to be speechless.

"You don't have to answer us right now," Thomas continued, "but you think real hard about your answer. Because from now until the city council meeting when the final vote on this issue is taken, we are going to contact every news outlet we can and provide them with these pictures and their locations. We will let them know that we are confused as to why the city would choose to uproot hardworking citizens and a long-established church when doing so is obviously unnecessary."

Michael stared at the photos for a few moments, then lifted his gaze to Thomas. "Where did you get these?"

"This is the digital age, Mr. Barclay. Any novice with a camera and time on his hands could have taken these photos. So, what I am asking is, how many people will soon become aware that this city has dozens of other viable options for this business district, but instead of using those, you've chosen to uproot an entire community?"

"Well...." Michael looked uncomfortable. "I can't promise you that anything will change, but...I will check out these locations."

"That's all we're asking, Mr. Barclay," Thomas said as he and Yvonne stood up and gathered their jackets. "I'm confident that once you've reviewed those areas, you will make the right recommendation to the town council." Without another word, they walked out of the office and headed to the parking lot.

Once they were in the car, Yvonne broke the silence. "You were awesome!" she cheered, leaning over to hug Thomas.

"Oh, please. Tell me that when I've accomplished something. I couldn't even get us a meeting with the mayor."

"But we were speaking directly with the man in charge of the project," Yvonne pointed out. "I think that's better." She leaned back in her seat and adjusted her seat belt. "This is going to work—I can feel it." A few weeks ago, when Toya had said that Thomas was her hero, Yvonne had ignored the comment. David had always been her hero, and she'd never wanted to give that title to another man. But day by day, as Thomas handled one thing after the next in order to make things easier for her, Yvonne was beginning to see exactly what Toya meant.

"Well, aren't we full of optimism today?" Thomas said with a grin.

"I'll admit that I was upset after speaking with your accountant. Who wouldn't be after learning that a trusted deacon had stolen four hundred thousand dollars—and then disappeared? To tell you the truth, I felt like I was being 'crucified.' And I was so drained that I fell asleep in my office chair—"

"Why didn't you just lie down on that comfortable sofa? Didn't you put that in your office for afternoon naps?" Thomas said, his grin mischievous now.

Yvonne playfully shoved his arm. "No, Thomas Reed, I did not put that sofa in my office just so I could take naps. It's for visitors. And I was trying to tell you something before I was rudely interrupted."

"Sorry. Continue."

"I guess God wanted to show me that I was throwing the word around a little too lightly, because when I fell asleep, I had a dream, and it was as if I had been carried back into ancient Roman times. I watched our Savior carry His cross. And I've got to tell you, He did a much better job of it than I'm doing."

Thomas put his hand on top of Yvonne's. "You're being too hard on yourself, Vonnie."

"I really don't think I am. Yes, a lot has happened to me in the past two years: my husband died, my church has been falling apart, my daughter got pregnant, my deacon was robbing the church...and now, someone is trying to take the church from us. But even though things are difficult, nobody's spitting in my face. No one is nailing me to a tree and murdering me without one just reason for his actions."

"When you put it like that, I guess that anything we have to go through doesn't seem so bad."

Yvonne knew that Thomas understood her. He was a godsend, and she hoped that she would always have his friendship. "It's like a wise man recently told me—this, too, shall pass." She smiled at Thomas as she repeated his own words. He was smiling back at her, but then his expression changed, and she saw hunger—need—in his eyes. Those beautiful hazel eyes were drawing her in. She leaned closer, in spite of her desire to stop because, if she leaned any closer, she knew they would kiss.

Yet she was powerless to retreat. It seemed that Thomas was under the same spell, too; although he hadn't said a word, she still saw the desire for her in his eyes. Yvonne inhaled the strong, manly scent of his cologne and was swept away with the sudden urge to devour this man.

Yvonne's phone rang, and the spell was broken. She looked at the caller ID and then said with shaky voice, "It's Toya. I was going to call and see where she was, but I forgot." She answered the phone. "Hey, hon! Are you okay?"

Thomas turned the key in the ignition and started to back his car out of the parking lot.

"Mom, I'm so sorry I missed the meeting," Toya said. "Are you still in with the mayor?"

"Actually, the mayor never showed up. We met with one of his assistants."

"You're kidding! I thought you told me that Dawn scheduled the appointment for the evening because that was the only time the mayor had available."

"That's what we were told, but apparently the mayor had more pressing business out of town. So, he sent the person in charge of the project...which was just as good as meeting with the mayor, or maybe even better, as far as I'm concerned. Thomas gave him a lot to think about, so I'm praying that this will work out in our favor."

"It will, Mama. Just keep on believing."

"Thanks, sweetie. So, what happened to you?"

"I went out to dinner with a friend, and when we left the restaurant, the valet couldn't find his car. We're at the police station now, filing a report. I just stepped out for a moment so I could call you."

"Who is this 'friend' you're out with?" Yvonne asked, trying to sound less concerned than she was.

"His name is Marvel Williams. Don't worry, Mama; he's a nice guy. He has his own company, and I really like him."

"So, when do I get to meet this wonderful man?"

"In two weeks—at the wedding."

"Toya, I think I should meet this man before you bring him all the way to the Bahamas, don't you?"

"Oh, no. You are way too critical of my boyfriends. This time, I want to make up my own mind. So, I will introduce you to him at the wedding, okay?"

"Whatever, Toya. I am not critical of anyone. I try to tell you girls what I see, and you just get mad because I'm usually right."

Changing the subject, Toya asked, "Did Uncle Thomas think the meeting went well?"

"He seems to be a little more skeptical on the matter than I am. But I truly think it was a slam dunk! Those people are going to be thinking twice about taking our church from us."

They reached Yvonne's house just as she wrapped up her conversation with Toya. Thomas pulled his car into her driveway and turned off the engine. "Before you go inside," he said, turning to face her, "I need to talk to you about something."

Yvonne took her hand off the door handle and looked at Thomas, hoping that he wasn't going to ask her about what almost happened between them. By now, she had come back to her senses and knew that kissing Thomas would have been the wrong thing to do. "What's up?"

"I know that you are in a happy place, believing everything will turn out all right. But I have some uneasy feelings."

"About what?"

"Well, I think we need to find out who this factory owner is, and why he's so interested in the church's land. Who knows? We might be sitting on an oil field or something."

She looked at him doubtfully. "In Detroit?"

"Okay, not oil, but there has to be some reason why these guys have picked our area of town to set up shop."

"Do you think we need to hire an investigator or something?" Yvonne asked.

"Yes, I do. And I want the investigator to find Clarence Brown for us. Do you have any objections?"

"No, Thomas. I think you're right. We need to know exactly what we're up against. Maybe if we find Deacon Brown, we'll also find some of our money."

"And we need to file a police report against Clarence now."

"Do you really think so? Can't it wait until we find him and hear his side of the story?"

Shaking his head, Thomas said, "We've waited too long as it is. We need to be proactive if we're going to get any of that money back."

"Okay, I'll take care of it tomorrow." She turned and grasped the door handle again.

"One more thing," he added, halting her again. "I talked to Fred Tompkins today, and he asked me if you had another book in the works. He said they're ready to publish it whenever it's available."

Yvonne pressed her palm to her brow and shook her head. "With everything that's going on right now, I just don't know when I would have the time to write another book."

"I think you should consider it, Yvonne," Thomas said gently. "Getting back into writing may help to take your mind off some of the things we're dealing with."

Although she didn't want to admit it, she liked the way he kept saying "we" and "us." They were a team, and she needed him in her life at this point in time. "I don't think I would be able to focus, Thomas. Tell Fred I said thanks for thinking of me, but right now, I've got a wedding to plan."

Chapter Twelve

*Y*VONNE HAD SPENT THE PAST TWO WEEKS FINALIZ-
ing all the details for Tia's destination wedding
in the Bahamas. She was thankful that it would be
just a small, intimate affair, for who knows how long
it would have taken her to plan a wedding for five
hundred-plus guests!

Meanwhile, Thomas had been working with a private investigator to find Clarence Brown, as well as
to uncover the identity of the entrepreneur who wanted to build his factory on the land where Christ-Life
Sanctuary currently resided. So far, no productive information about Clarence had turned up, but the investigator had finally found out that the factory owner
was a man by the name of Edward M. Williams. The
last name rang a bell with Yvonne for some reason,
but with everything that was going on, she couldn't
figure out where she had heard it or why it seemed
significant.

Thomas had tried to make an appointment with
the man, but Mr. Williams's office had informed him
that the owner would be out of the country for a week.
So, Thomas had set up an appointment for the day
after Yvonne and he would return from the Bahamas.

Since they couldn't get ahold of the factory owner
until they returned to the States, Yvonne made up her
mind to just relax and enjoy her daughter's wedding.

For the ceremony, Dawn had found a private beach that featured a beach house for the wedding party to get ready. She'd also reserved a nearby reception hall, where the twenty-five guests could celebrate before heading over to the Atlantis to spend the night.

The groom had invited his parents, his two sisters, three of his cousins, and two of his best friends from college. The rest of the guests were close friends of Tia's.

As the color scheme, Tia had chosen ivory and aqua, so Yvonne had purchased a long, formfitting teal dress that actually looked good on her. When Tia had first told her the colors she'd selected, Yvonne had been worried. Aqua was not her favorite color, but the teal complemented her light skin tone surprisingly well.

With less than an hour until the beachfront ceremony, she left her hotel room to catch a cab over to the other side of the island where the wedding would take place. She was immediately assaulted by the heat as she stepped out of the air-conditioned hotel, and she rushed past the hotel attendant to the cab, praying that the driver had the air on full blast.

As she was about to get into the cab, Thomas called out to her, "Yvonne, am I glad I caught you!" He jogged over and opened the back passenger door for her, then slid in next to her. "We need to talk."

"Who didn't do what this time?" Yvonne asked, pulling a tissue out of her purse to dab at the perspiration on her forehead. Tia had been complaining almost nonstop since they'd arrived the previous morning. The florist hadn't sent the right color of flowers (as if there were that many different shades of aqua). Also, the caterers' menu was not up to par, the DJ's song list was lacking, and she feared that her tummy showed too much in her dress. Yvonne couldn't take another complaint from her daughter's mouth, and she had rather enjoyed the solitude while getting dressed in her hotel room.

"This isn't about Tia," Thomas said. He sighed. "We have a problem with Toya."

She looked at Thomas as if he had suddenly grown two heads. "What did that girl do?"

"Well, I guess the problem is not with Toya, exactly. It's more like we have a problem with the man Toya is dating."

"Marvel? I met him last night. He seems harmless enough. At least he has a job, which is more than I can say for my soon-to-be son-in-law."

"I probably shouldn't have said anything about this before the wedding, but something just doesn't seem right to me. I mean, if he knew that he would see us this weekend, why didn't he simply meet with me last week instead of putting me off?"

"Thomas, what are you babbling about?"

He turned to face her. "Marvel is Edward M. Williams."

"I still don't understand what has you so upset."

"Marvel—he's the man who wants to build a factory on the land where Christ-Life Sanctuary sits."

With all that had been going on recently, Yvonne's attention span had become very short. She shook her head. "I met Marvel last night. He's a nice guy. There's no way he has anything to do with trying to tear down our church."

"It's him, Yvonne."

"How can you be sure?"

"Because when I met him this morning, I thought I recognized him. But I didn't say anything because I wasn't sure. I went back to my hotel room and called the private investigator. I had him fax me another copy of Edward M. Williams's picture. It was a match. Then I called Mr. Williams's office, and his assistant informed me that Mr. Williams was in the Bahamas and could not be reached until he returned to the States next week."

Yvonne's eyebrows shot up and her mouth hung open. When she was finally able to form a coherent phrase, she said, "Are you telling me that Toya is dating the man who is trying to destroy our church?"

"I don't know if he thinks of what he's doing in that manner, but yes, she is dating the man who wants our land." Thomas paused. "He's already at the beach house with Toya. When I get over there, I'm going to get some answers out of him."

"Do you think it's a coincidence that the man dating my daughter is the same man who wants to build a factory on our land?"

"I certainly don't. I think Mr. Williams is playing some type of game, and we need to figure out the rules as quickly as possible."

When they arrived at the beach house, Yvonne and Thomas couldn't get out of the cab fast enough. The driver yelled, "Hey, you must pay!"

Thomas ducked his head inside the vehicle, pulled a few bills out of his pocket, and handed them to the driver. "Sorry about that. My mind is on other things."

The driver smiled at the cash in his hand. "No problem at all. You call me if you need a ride back." The man handed Thomas a business card.

Yvonne left Thomas with the cab driver. The moment she'd gotten out of the car, she'd spotted Toya and Marvel on the front porch of the beach house, wrapped in an embrace and whispering into each other's ears.

"Get away from my daughter!" she shouted as she started up the dozen porch steps, taking them two at a time.

Toya looked startled and broke away from Marvel. "Mama, what's wrong?" she asked, her eyebrows arched in confusion.

Yvonne reached the top step, and she started wagging her finger as she stormed over to Marvel. "I don't know what kind of sick game you think you're playing with my family, but you will leave my daughter alone this instant."

Thomas bounded up the steps and maneuvered his way in front of Yvonne. "I need to speak with you for a moment, Marvel," he said.

"What's this all about?" Toya demanded.

"This man is trying to take the land that our church sits on," Yvonne said matter-of-factly.

Thomas grabbed Marvel's arm and took him inside while Yvonne and Toya stayed on the porch.

"Mama, why would you go and embarrass me like this?" Toya asked. "Now do you see why I didn't want to introduce you to him?"

"Honey, listen to me," Yvonne said, praying for composure. "This man is not who you think he is. He is trying to take our church away from us. Just ask yourself why he would be dating you when he knows full well that what he's doing will hurt us all."

"Marvel is a good guy, Mama. He has nothing to do with whatever is going on at the church. Your beef is with the City of Detroit, not Marvel Williams."

"His name is *Edward* Marvel Williams. Did he ever tell you that?"

"No, but what difference does it make? Plenty of people go by their middle name."

It appeared that Toya was going to defend this man until the bitter end. "He's no good, baby. He's got ulterior motives for wanting to be with you," Yvonne said, shaking her head.

"Oh, so, if some fine-looking, intelligent, wealthy man wants to be with me, he must have some reason other than the simple fact that he enjoys my company."

"Toya, any man would be blessed and privileged to have you—just not this man. Okay? I'm not sure exactly what's going on here, but this can't be a coincidence. You're a lawyer, hon, so look at the facts. Did this man start dating you around the same time he began looking for land to build his factory?"

Toya was quiet for a moment, but then she said, "I don't see how that makes any difference. So what if he was looking for land? It's not as if I could—or would—help him take our church's land."

Before Yvonne could say another word, Tia came running out onto the porch. She was wearing her white satin tea-length wedding dress with pearl beads shimmering all over the bodice. Her veil was outlined in pearls. Yvonne almost lost her breath to see her baby daughter looking so radiant.

"Mama, thank goodness you're here! I was getting worried."

Yvonne opened her arms and gave Tia a hug. "You look beautiful, sweetheart. Simply beautiful."

"You don't think my dress is too short?" Tia asked.

Yvonne stepped back and studied her daughter. The dress was dazzling yet fun. "I like long wedding gowns, but you're getting married on a beach, so I think the short dress works."

Tia hugged Yvonne again. "Thanks, Mama." She turned to Toya. "Can you get everyone ready so we can go down to the beach and get this wedding over with?"

"Sure, little sis. I'll take care of everything." Toya turned back to her mother and asked, "Can we squash this until after the wedding?"

A gust of wind billowed the feather-like palm fronds in the trees around them, and in the surf, white, flaky pebbles were thrown against the beach. Surrounded by such beauty, Yvonne suddenly didn't want to argue anymore. Tia looked gorgeous in her wedding dress, and Toya looked pretty in her aqua, tea-length bridesmaid dress, even though the color was not the best for her. "Let's do this wedding," Yvonne said with as much joy as she could muster.

Robbie—or Robert Samuel Carter, as his name read on the programs—was not where he was supposed to be. During the rehearsal last night, Robbie had been told to wait for Yvonne in front of the chairs on the right side of the arch. But he wasn't there right now. So, the wedding coordinator, Barbara, told Yvonne to take her place behind the arch, and she went to look for him. Soft music began to play. It sounded like live piano, but there was no instrument in sight. Yvonne finally spotted the small, discreet speakers arranged around the chairs.

She glanced up and saw Toya at the end of the aisle, preparing to walk toward the front. Tia was right behind her, holding onto Thomas's arm. He reached over and wiped what must have been a tear from her cheek.

Yvonne wished David could be here to wipe the tears from Tia's cheeks. But he was gone, and she had to face the fact and move on. Just then, she was struck by how handsome Thomas looked in his black tuxedo. The man could dazzle.

Barbara came running back down the beach toward them. That's when Yvonne saw Robbie. His best man and one of his cousins were holding him up and carrying him a few paces behind the wedding coordinator.

"What's going on?" Yvonne asked no one in particular.

With no explanation, Barbara changed the song that was playing through the speakers and then said something to Toya, who began to walk down the aisle carrying her pretty bouquet. Robbie finally made his way to his spot in front of the arch, but not without the help of his best man, who held Robbie's arm, even when he stood still.

Yvonne turned her attention from Robbie to Tia, who glowed as she walked down the aisle. Yvonne's baby daughter was in love, and she was finally ready to accept the entire situation. What else could she do? In a few minutes, her baby would be married, and a few months later, Tia would be a mommy with a baby of her own. Tia smiled at her, and Yvonne felt as if her heart would explode with all the love she had for her daughter at that moment.

Then, Robbie fell down. Yvonne saw him out of the corner of her eye. Her attention shot back to the aisle, though, as Tia let go of Thomas's arm and ran to her man. She and the best man tried to get Robbie back up, but Robbie fought against their efforts. He pushed them away and said, "I can do it," but his words were so slurred that it sounded like he said, "I kum d'i."

Tia was crying again, but this time, her tears were not of joy or happiness. "Why did you do this?" she screamed at Robbie.

Robbie tried to stand up. "I—I—I g-g-got th-this," he stammered as he grabbed Tia's arm and turned her toward Yvonne. "Let's do th-this." Then, he fell down again.

Some of the guests gasped, but others sat in their seats with smiles on their faces as if nothing was wrong. Their behavior made Yvonne think of the people who had stood around watching Christ's crucifixion even though they knew he'd done nothing to deserve it. Or, the people who knew that the Holocaust and slavery were wrong but did not feel compelled to speak out against them. Yvonne's mother used to tell her that plenty of cowards will always sit around and watch bad things happen; it takes just one honorable person to stand up and do something about it.

"This boy is drunk," Yvonne stated, pointing at Robbie.

Tia bent down and tried to pick up her groom again. When it was obvious that she wouldn't be able to, Thomas picked him up and sat him in a chair.

Tia turned back to Yvonne and said, "I don't know what happened to him. He was fine last night. Please, Mama, just marry us, and I'll take him back to the hotel and let him sleep it off."

Yvonne put her hands on her hips. "I am not about to marry you to a drunk. Have you lost your mind?" Yvonne wanted to strike out and hit Robbie. There was no way she would officiate this marriage.

"But Mama!" Tia cried. "I have to get married!" She looked out at the guests, then turned back to her mother and whispered, "You know why I have to get married today. Please do this for me."

Yvonne felt sorry for Tia and her situation, and her daughter's tears did have an effect on her. But Yvonne was a woman of God, and she would not marry any couple who came before the altar of God drunk—especially not when the sober one was her baby girl. "I can't do it, hon. I'm sorry."

Tia turned to Thomas. "Will you please marry us, Uncle Thomas?" she begged. "I need to get married. I know Robbie's drunk right now, but he's really a good guy." She grabbed Robbie's hand and tried to pull him up once more.

Instead of standing up, Robbie fell off the chair.

A look of remorse crossed Thomas's face, but he said, "I agree with your mother, Tia. I would never marry you under these conditions."

Tia dropped Robbie's hand and ran away. Toya threw down her flowers and followed her sister.

Yvonne turned to the small gathering of guests. "I'm sorry, but there will be no wedding here today. Please feel free to enjoy the food that has already been prepared for you in the reception hall."

Thomas whispered in her ear, "I'm going to take Robbie back to the beach house, and then I'll be back for you."

"Just get him out of my face." She had had enough.

Thomas patted her shoulder, then bent down to help the best man lift Robbie up, and Robbie thanked him by throwing up all over his tuxedo.

Chapter Thirteen

THINGS QUIETED DOWN AFTER YVONNE USHERED THE guests into the reception hall to get out of the heat and humidity and feast on hors d'oeuvres and the buffet dinner. She had a splitting headache and wanted desperately to go back to the hotel and lie down. But with Tia, Toya, and Thomas absent, she felt obligated to stay at the reception hall and entertain the guests.

She was thankful that there were only about twenty people at the reception. She probably would have been in a daze if there had been two hundred or more people to put on a face for after the botched wedding ceremony.

"Are you okay, Mrs. Milner?" someone asked. Yvonne turned, shocked to see Marvel Williams standing beside her. She hadn't seen him approaching. "You look a bit flustered."

"I'm fine," she replied, "but I'm not so sure that you should be here, Mr. Williams."

"Please, call me Marvel. And I'm not your enemy, Mrs. Milner."

He was smiling as he spoke to her, but Yvonne saw something else in his eyes. Something akin to hatred. But Yvonne didn't know this young man. What reason could he have for hating her? "It feels like you're my enemy, Mr. Williams, because I don't understand why

you would insist on taking land that is already occupied when you could build your factory in one of so
many other locations within the city of Detroit."

"See, I think this is where we're getting our wires
crossed, because I didn't insist on taking any land,"
Marvel explained. "I told the city which areas I was
most interested in and the size my organization would
be when construction was finished, and they came
back with a location. But I had no idea that your
church would be in jeopardy."

He sounded so convincing, Yvonne almost believed
him. But then she recalled that the mayor's assistant
had told them that Marvel specifically requested the
location where Christ-Life sat. So, somebody was lying, and Yvonne figured that she was looking at the
liar. But Toya was dating this man. For her daughter's
sake, Yvonne needed to keep the peace. So, she said,
"I hope that what you say is the truth, Mr. Williams.
My daughter seems to believe you, so I am willing to
reserve judgment until I have all the facts."

"I appreciate that, Mrs. Milner. And for the record, I
really like Toya and wouldn't dream of doing anything
to hurt her."

"I hope that's true, Marvel," Thomas said as he
walked up and stood next to Yvonne. "Because having
Christ-Life Sanctuary torn down would definitely hurt
Toya."

"Mr. Reed," Marvel said, extending his hand. Thomas did likewise, and they shook hands. "Toya speaks
very highly of you, sir," Marvel continued. "It's nice
to finally get a chance to speak with you. I know you
called my office to schedule a meeting, and if you'd
like, we can sit down now and chat."

"Right now is not a good time for me, Marvel. Why don't we just keep our appointment next week, and then we can sit down and talk this all out?"

"Okay, then," Marvel said. "I'll talk to you about this when we get back to Detroit."

Thomas turned to Yvonne. "Would you like to escape with me for a moment?" he asked her.

Yvonne looked around the room at the guests, who were sitting around and eating their expensive lunch. "I think I need to stay here and make sure no one needs anything."

"I've already told Barbara to let everyone know that I'm covering one night's stay at the hotel for all of them, and that their dinner is on me, too. So, I think they will be all right if we disappear for a few minutes."

Why hadn't Yvonne thought of letting Barbara handle the guests? After all, she was the wedding coordinator, and she had already been paid for the services she would render during the weekend. "Thanks, Thomas. If I had remembered about Barbara, I would already be back in my hotel room."

Thomas turned back to Marvel. "Enjoy the rest of your day. Dinner and your hotel room are on me. We'll talk to you later."

With that, he took Yvonne by the arm and guided her outside.

"I'm so drained," Yvonne admitted. "I just want to go to my room and lie down."

"I know. But before you do that, I want you to take a walk with me."

"I guess I can walk with you for a few minutes. There's something I wanted to tell you, anyway."

They started walking toward the beach but stopped to take off their shoes. Thomas was still wearing his tuxedo pants and shirt, but he had left the soiled jacket in the reception hall.

Yvonne took off her pumps and buried her toes in the cool sand. It felt wonderful, and for a moment she forgot about the debacle at the ceremony.

"So, what did you want to talk to me about?" Thomas asked as they resumed walking.

Yvonne kicked a pile of white sand. "I appreciate your offer to pay for the hotel stay and dinner for Tia's guests, but I can't let you do that. I'll take care of the costs."

Thomas stopped walking and turned to face Yvonne. "Why can't you let me pay for this? I'm the one who suggested that Tia and Robbie get married in the Bahamas in the first place. I'm going to pay for those rooms and those meals, and I'm not listening to any arguments about it. So, just smile and say thank you."

"You aren't Tia's father, Thomas. You shouldn't have to spend your money on her mistakes."

"I'm still waiting for you to say thank you...."

She shoved him playfully. "Thomas, why do you have to be so sweet to us? Can't you find some other dysfunctional family to lavish your kindness on?"

"I wouldn't have this much fun with anyone else," he said with a hint of laughter in his eyes.

Yvonne locked arms with him, and they began to walk again. "How did things get so messed up?" she wondered aloud. "When Tia told me a few weeks ago that Robbie was fired because his boss thought he'd come to work drunk, I should have known something was up. But Tia swore that it was cold medicine that had made Robbie act drunk."

"Well, we know he wasn't drinking cold medicine today," Thomas said. "But let's just wait and hear what the kids have to say when this all blows over."

Yvonne headed for a pine tree on the beach, and she lowered herself onto the sand as Thomas sat down next to her. "I already know what they want to do," Yvonne said. "Tia still wants to marry him. Did you see the way she looked at me when I told her that I wouldn't marry them?"

"Now, don't go taking it personally. Tia's not upset with you, Vonnie. She's probably mad at herself for getting into this predicament in the first place."

"Thomas, do you know who you're talking about? She's my daughter, but I know how self-absorbed she is. At this very minute, Tia is trying to find someone to blame for this disaster, and I promise you, she won't be blaming herself."

"I don't know about that. I went back to the hotel with Robbie, remember? Well, Tia came to be with him, and she was pretty broken up. I saw something in her eyes that made me believe that these events have changed her."

"Why didn't you tell me that before? I need to go see about my baby." Yvonne tried to get up, but Thomas held her arm.

"Toya is taking care of Tia. You just sit back down here and let me take care of you."

Yvonne started to get back up again, but then she relented. Thomas was right. She did need a moment to herself. She had almost been at the breaking point in the reception hall, just trying to hold it together so that she wouldn't give the guests anything else to whisper about. She closed her eyes and leaned her head on Thomas's shoulder. "Thank you for being here, Thomas. You always know exactly what I need."

"It's in my job description. Something like: 'a lowly assistant pastor has to take care of the senior pastor and anticipate her every need.'"

"Hush up, Thomas! There is nothing lowly about you. And you're not the assistant pastor. We are copastoring the church as equals."

"If you say so, boss."

Giggling, Yvonne poked him in the side with her elbow. "Stop that. You are worse than the kids."

"I'm just trying to make you laugh. The Bible says, *'A merry heart does good, like medicine.'*"

She lifted her head off his shoulder and turned to face her friend. "I have been in need of that particular medicine for a while now. But with my younger daughter wanting to marry a drunk and my older daughter dating the man who's trying to take the church away from us, I just haven't found much to laugh about."

"It's tough watching your kids grow up and having to back off and let them make their own mistakes. A little while ago, when I met Jarrod for breakfast, he was trying to talk to this young lady, and I instantly knew she was all wrong for him. But do you think he listened to me? Nope! He and this girl have been on three dates since then."

"When they get too grown to listen to parental counsel, we should still be able to lock them in their rooms or something," Yvonne put in. "I mean, look at Toya. She is a very intelligent woman. Men ask her out all the time. But the one she picks is a church destroyer."

"We can't call him a church destroyer just yet—we still don't know for sure if Marvel is directing the action against the church, or if it's coming straight from the mayor's office."

"Thomas, why would the mayor be behind something like this? Christ-Life has been in the same spot for two decades, and no city official has ever sought to move us off of our land before now."

"Detroit is in desperate need of new businesses right now," Thomas reminded her.

"Yes, of course it is. And I could believe that the desperation the mayor's office is feeling about economic growth is the reason they are willing to uproot us. But I still don't believe it was their idea."

"You might be right. But why is Marvel so interested in our particular side of town?"

"I don't know, but I intend to find out."

Thomas leaned over and put an arm around Yvonne's shoulders. "We will figure it out together," he said, sounding determined.

Yvonne's breath caught in her throat. Her heart thumped loudly in her chest as her blood pressure raced. Thomas had put his arm around her shoulder at least a hundred times through the years, and his touch had never made her feel like this. She was nervous and unsure of her emotions.

Thomas must have sensed her reaction. "What's wrong?" he asked, his eyes boring into hers.

You're too close for comfort, that's what's wrong, Yvonne wanted to tell him. But how could she explain to a man who had been her friend for so many years that she had strange, new feelings for him? She couldn't tell him what was wrong, so she turned her face away from him.

"Vonnie," he said with a husky voice. "I feel it, too."

With that funny feeling still in her stomach, she turned back to face him. She looked into his eyes and saw the desire she had seen several weeks ago. What was she supposed to do? Her answer came quickly as Thomas leaned closer to her and touched his lips to hers. The kiss was awkward at first. Yvonne hadn't kissed any man but David in thirty years, so it took her a moment to get used to the feel of Thomas's mouth.

Then, what had started as a gentle kiss became ravenous. They were like two hungry people receiving their first meal after a two-year fast. Yvonne didn't want the kiss to end, but at the same time, she wanted to end it. She was so confused that she couldn't wrap her mind around what was going on or the sensations she was feeling. She pulled away from Thomas. "What are we doing?"

"I don't know, but it feels right to me, Vonnie. It feels real right," Thomas said as he reclaimed her lips.

When the kiss started up again, Yvonne forgot to think. Thomas held her in his arms and took her breath away with the amazing way he kissed her. Then, he suddenly stood up and held out his hand to her.

"Come on. Let's go check on the girls, and then I'm taking you out on the town."

"W-what?" she asked, confused by his sudden urgency.

"We have to go, Vonnie. As much as I would love to stay here kissing on you all day, we need to make sure the girls are okay. And then I need to get some food in your stomach, because I know you haven't eaten anything all day."

Oh, yeah—the girls. Yvonne grasped Thomas's hand and allowed him to pull her to her feet. As she brushed the sand off her dress, she tried to clear her head so that she could think rationally again. "I guess we'd better go check on the girls," she agreed, because the silence was beginning to get awkward.

As they walked hand in hand toward the reception hall, Yvonne had her mind set on getting back to the Atlantis, dealing with Tia and Toya, and then figuring out whatever this was that was happening between her and Thomas.

From his position behind a big palm tree just a few feet away from Thomas and Yvonne, Marvel snapped pictures of their intimate moment with his cell phone. He reveled in his good fortune. Technology was something else, and he wanted to kiss the person who had come up with the idea of cell phones equipped with cameras and video recorders. No one had noticed him taping that crazy scene at the wedding, which would be an instant hit on YouTube. And he was getting ready to send these pictures of the good reverend, Pastor Yvonne Milner, to all of the newspapers, television stations, and radio talk shows that he could find in Detroit. Maybe the producers at CNN would be as interested in this as they were in Yvonne's sob story.

The film from the wedding would embarrass Pastor Yvonne, but this little lovebird scene was going to destroy her. She was about to lose all credibility, and soon, City Council wouldn't listen to a word she had to say. Marvel was confident that his project would now go through.

Just think—if he hadn't been willing to take the risk and follow the two lovebirds out here, he never would have received all the ammunition he needed to shut them up and get his plans moving forward again. If he were a God-fearing man, he might even thank the good Lord right now. But he hadn't been in a thankful mood in a long time. That would soon change, however. He was sure of it.

Chapter Fourteen

THOMAS HAD PLANNED TO TAKE YVONNE OUT TO DIN-
ner after they'd checked on the girls. But when
they arrived back at the hotel, they had more on
their hands than they had bargained for, and Thomas decided simply to order room service. Before that,
though, his first order of business was to get Tia,
Toya, Robbie, and Robbie's brother Mike out of the
hotel lobby. They were screaming at each other at the
top of their lungs, and hotel security had been called.
"I need everybody to quiet down!" Thomas shouted
above the melee.

The angry group turned to him, and all of them
started talking at once, trying to explain.

"I said, be quiet!" Thomas commanded them again.
He then turned to the hotel manager, who had just
arrived on the scene. "I apologize for the disorderly
conduct of this group. I'm going to take them to my
suite, where I'm sure we will be able to settle things in
a peaceful manner."

The hotel manager nodded, then looked at Tia, still
wearing her wedding dress. Streaks of black mascara
ran down her face from all the crying she'd been doing. "I'm sorry things didn't go well today," he said to
Thomas.

"Thank you," Thomas replied, and then he ushered
Yvonne and everyone else to the elevator. Once they

were in his room, he had to order the young people to be silent yet again. "Your mother hasn't eaten a thing all day," he told Tia and Toya, "and I need to order some food before we get into this matter."

He called room service and ordered a seafood platter that could serve ten people, then sat down on the couch next to Yvonne. "Now, can someone please tell us why you all were carrying on in the lobby if as you had no home training at all?" Then he looked at Robbie and said, "You already showed us that you have no home training at the wedding, but these girls were not much better."

"I wasn't trying to cause trouble," Robbie insisted.

Thomas ignored him and turned back to the girls. "Now, I know that you're grown women, and that you can get yourselves arrested, if you want to. But do you have any concern for your mother?"

"Of course we do, Uncle Thomas," Toya said, placing her hands on her hips. "But Robbie was trying to blame Marvel for his own drunken behavior, and that's just not right."

Tia pointed an accusatory finger at Robbie. "This jerk is trying to blame someone else for his own out-of-control behavior." Tears flowed down her face as she continued. "You ruined my wedding, Robbie. I will never forgive you for that."

"It was my wedding, too, Tia. And I promise you that I didn't get plastered on purpose. Marvel put something in my drink, I swear."

"Marvel handed you a Pepsi. I saw him do it myself," Toya retorted.

Evidently not willing to go down without a fight, Robbie countered, "Yeah, but he whispered in my ear that he had filled the can with beer. He said that he could tell I needed to relax. So, I took it. But that was the only thing I had to drink all morning. If I got that drunk on one beer, then he must have mixed something else with it."

Now Tia had her hands on her hips. "So, what you're telling us is, you knew full well that you were drinking beer on the morning of our wedding, and you did it, anyway? How does that make this not your fault, Robbie?"

He tried to walk toward Tia, but when she balled her fist and got in a fighting stance, he backed up. "Okay, okay, I was wrong for drinking the beer. But I was all wound up. I was nervous about reciting our vows."

Tia's eyes widened. "You weren't really drinking cough medicine that day you got fired, were you? My mother asked me if you had a drinking problem, and I swore to her that you didn't. And look how you repay my trust—you humiliate me on what is supposed to be the most wonderful day of my life." She crossed her arms over her chest and turned her back to him.

Robbie looked at Thomas, his expression distraught. "Help me out here, Mr. Reed. I swear I didn't do this on purpose."

Thomas almost believed the young man. His eyes were so full of sorrow and fear. Thomas truly believed that Robbie was afraid of losing Tia's love, and right now, it looked like that was exactly what was about to happen. But what could he do? If Robbie had a drinking problem and Tia had married him, he would have ruined her life. So, he looked Robbie in the eye and said, "Here's my problem. I'm bothered by the fact that you drink. Do you really think that you can be a good example for your wife and future child with a drinking problem?"

"I don't have a drinking problem, sir. I made a mistake, that's all," Robbie said.

Tia rolled her eyes and let out a loud sigh.

Mike stepped forward and said his first words since they'd entered Thomas's suite. "You do have a drinking problem, Robbie. I have one, too." He turned to look at Tia. "Robbie was drinking that day he got fired. I know because we were drinking together."

Robbie shoved his brother. "Why are you turnin' on me like this? You ain't right. You're just jealous of what I have with Tia."

Mike shoved him back. "You need help, man. We both do."

The brothers grabbed each other as if they were in a wrestling match and began trying to pull each other down.

"What in the world?" Yvonne said as she jumped up from the couch.

Thomas got in the middle of the fight and managed to pull the two apart somehow. "Look! This is my hotel room, and I'm not about to pay for any damages the two of you may cause. So, I suggest you stop this foolishness and listen to me for a minute."

There was a knock at the door. Thomas turned to Yvonne. "Can you get that? I'm sure it's our food." He looked back at Robbie and Mike and said, "Sit down."

The brothers took a seat on the couch.

Thomas grabbed his wallet, hurried over to the door, and handed the waiter a tip. Yvonne and the girls carried the food over to the dining room table, leaving Thomas in the living room area to talk with the men. "Now, Mike, you acknowledged that you need help with your drinking problem. And if you're serious, I can show you how to get the help you need."

"Show Robbie, too," Tia called out from the dining room, amid the sounds of cracking crab legs.

"He has to want the help, Tia, and so far, Robbie hasn't admitted that he has a problem," Thomas replied. He turned his attention back to Mike. "Now, the help I'm talking about comes through knowing Jesus Christ. Are you ready for that kind of help, Mike?"

"I was baptized when I was a kid, but that hasn't done anything for me. I still keep drinking."

Thomas put a hand on Mike's shoulder. "Son, baptism is important, but sometimes people put the cart before the horse. What I'm trying to tell you is that baptism is an outward showing of the cleansing that has already taken place on the inside. So, if God hasn't come into your heart, you might as well not even get baptized. Just go swim in the lake with a bunch of your friends if you feel the need to get dunked."

With a look of confusion on his face, Mike said, "I don't understand."

"What I'm trying to tell you is this: if you want your life to change for the better, then you need to invite Jesus Christ to come into your heart. I can show you how to do that if you're ready."

Mike sent his brother a questioning look, but Robbie only shrugged. Mike turned back to Thomas and said, "I want to know Jesus. Can you show me how to invite Him into my heart?"

"Yes, I can," Thomas said.

He instructed Mike to stand up. Once they were face-to-face, Thomas led the young man in the sinner's prayer. Mike repeated the words and declared that he was a sinner, recognized Jesus as the Son of God, and Jesus' death, burial, and resurrection as real, and then claimed the power of the resurrection for himself.

When the prayer was over, tears flowed down Mike's face as he jumped around the room, declaring that he was free. He then turned to Thomas and asked, "Can you baptize me again, sir? I want the whole world to know that something has happened on the inside of me." He pumped his hands in the air and shouted, "I can feel it!"

Robbie sat on the couch, watching his brother but saying nothing. Thomas didn't push. He knew that every man must count up the cost for his own salvation, and that right now, the cost must seem too high for Robbie. So, he called nonchalantly to the women, "I hope you ladies haven't eaten all the food, because we men are starving, too."

"We sure are!" Robbie shouted, jumping up from the couch and racing into the dining room.

Thomas and Mike followed him in, and Thomas saw Tia glare at Robbie as he sat down next to her.

"What'd I do now?" Robbie asked.

"Nothing, Robbie. Don't you even worry about it," Tia said snidely.

Yvonne was in awe of Thomas. He'd seen the hurt in Mike's eyes and had done something about it. She had been too busy sitting on the couch, trying not to say a word to anybody. She'd had enough and just wanted to go to her room and lie down. But Thomas had shown her that God could still bring about a miracle even in the midst of dysfunction. He had been about his Father's business, just as the Bible instructed in 1 Peter 3:15: *"But sanctify the Lord God in your hearts, and always be ready to give a defense to everyone who asks you a reason for the hope that is in you, with meekness and fear."*

When Thomas had invited Mike to come to Detroit and attend church the following Sunday to be baptized, Yvonne had wanted to ask why he didn't simply use the tub in his hotel room—*If the boy wants to be baptized, let's get on with it!* But then she'd realized that Thomas had reasons for putting it off until church. "Invite your family, and I'll take everyone to dinner next Sunday after we get you baptized," he'd said.

Yvonne understood now. She turned to Robbie and said, "You're more than welcome to attend the baptism next week."

Robbie looked at Tia. "Do you mind if I come?"

"It is no longer any of my concern what you do, Robbie Carter. I wouldn't care if you jumped off a bridge." With that, Tia got up from her seat and rushed out of Thomas's suite.

Yvonne stood up. "I'll go talk to her. You all just continue what you're doing."

Toya got up, too. "I need to go check on Marvel."

Yvonne headed out of the room and found Tia running down the corridor. "Tia, stop! Wait."

When Tia turned and saw her mother, she ran back toward her and fell into her open arms. "I'm so stupid, I'm so stupid," she chanted as tears of sorrow and regret rolled down her face.

Toya walked slowly toward them, but Yvonne waved her away. "Come on, honey. Let me take you to my room so we can sit down and talk."

When they reached her room, Yvonne opened the door, and Tia went straight for the bed and lay down—the very thing Yvonne had wanted to do all afternoon.

Tears were still flowing down Tia's face. "What am I going to do, Mama?" she wailed.

Yvonne kicked off her shoes and climbed into bed next to her daughter. "The first thing we're going to do is pray. I need to ask God to forgive me for being so angry with Robbie that I failed to see his need for Christ." Thomas's actions that evening had reminded Yvonne that as a Christian, she didn't get to carry a grudge—not even when the offender had broken her baby girl's heart. "And you need to ask for forgiveness for doing things your own way instead of allowing God to guide you."

Tia wrapped her arms around Yvonne, just as she used to do when she was a little girl snuggling with her mommy in bed. "I know I messed up, Mama. I fell in love with Robbie so quick that I never even took time to find out if he had the same beliefs as me. I have made such a mess of my life—and my baby's life, too, and she's not even born."

Yvonne was amazed to hear her daughter admit that she had messed up. For once, Tia wasn't trying to lay blame on everybody but herself. Thomas had been right when he'd said that this incident would help Tia to grow.

They prayed together, and then Yvonne said, "Hon, I know that you are angry at Robbie right now. But the two of you will have to work together to raise that baby."

Tia's voice was calm as she said, "I know, Mom. But to tell you the truth, I don't know if I can forgive him for this."

"Earlier today, you were begging me to marry the two of you even though he was drunk. If I had done that, Robbie would be your husband right now, and you certainly wouldn't get anywhere by holding unforgiveness against him then. What makes you think it's okay to do so now?"

"I didn't want to marry him in that condition. I was just embarrassed. But now? I mean, look at all the money you and Uncle Thomas have wasted."

"We did spend a lot of money for a wedding that never took place. But Tia, honey, Thomas and I would much rather have you discover that Robbie has a drinking problem before you married him than after, no matter the cost."

"It's so embarrassing, Mama. I actually believed him about the cold medicine. I thought his boss was a real jerk for firing him. How stupid am I?"

"You're not stupid, sweetheart; you're just in love. And when we're in love, we want to believe everything our loved one says."

"I know you're probably thinking about Daddy right now. But, Mama, you had good reason to trust him."

"You're right about that. The only lie that man ever told me was about something he couldn't control—when he promised not to die on me." At that moment, Yvonne realized something. She had just been telling Tia that she would have to forgive Robbie for what he'd done; meanwhile, she hadn't truly "forgiven" David for dying on her.

"I'm tired, Mama. Do you mind if I sleep here for a while?"

"Not at all, baby girl. This king-size bed is more than big enough for both of us. I think I'm going to take a nap, as well." Yvonne turned over on her side, and a tear fell on her pillow as she whispered, "I forgive you, David. Rest in peace."

Chapter Fifteen

YVONNE MAY HAVE FALLEN ASLEEP THINKING ABOUT her husband, but she awoke with Thomas on her mind. The man was simply amazing. He was turning her world upside down and causing her to think of him more than she wanted to admit. But how could she help herself? Every time she turned around, Thomas was doing or saying something that caused her to feel privileged to know him. The man could go anywhere on earth and probably be welcomed with open arms, yet he'd chosen to stay with her. That counted for something, and she wanted to make sure Thomas knew that she recognized his worth.

Yvonne had planned to sit him down and tell him everything she was feeling when they returned to Detroit. However, she never got the chance. After the plane touched down, the moment Yvonne stepped into the airport, she was mobbed by swarms of reporters, all wanting to know how long she had been carrying on her affair with the world-renowned motivational speaker Thomas Reed.

"What?" was all Yvonne could say to the allegation. She was blinded by camera lights as one microphone after another was shoved in her face. She fought her way to her car, then fought her way to her front door, slamming it shut once she was safely inside.

"What in the world is going on?" she wondered out loud. Then, her phone rang.

Yvonne picked up the phone, and before she could even say hello, the female voice on the other end said, "Pastor Yvonne, can you tell me, did you know that Robert Carter was an alcoholic when he proposed to your daughter?"

"What?" Yvonne said, just as dumbfounded as she'd been while being attacked by the swarm of reporters.

"The video of the wedding is on YouTube, ma'am. It's gone viral, and everybody is talking about it."

Yvonne remained silent as this bit of information sank in.

"You didn't know?" the woman asked, her voice almost compassionate.

"I've been out of the country. I just got back in town. I'm going to have to check out some things before I can make any type of statement," Yvonne responded mechanically.

"That's fine, Pastor Yvonne, but can you tell me how long your relationship with Thomas Reed has been going on? He is quite a notable figure, so when pictures of him in a lip-lock with you surfaced, of course the news media went wild. And I'd just like to know if I could get an exclusive interview."

Yvonne hung up the phone and then sat down on the couch as she tried to make sense of the nightmare that was unfolding in front of her. Someone at the wedding must have filmed Robbie falling all over the place, throwing up, and then passing out. And then another person had taken pictures of her and Thomas as they kissed—or did the same person do both? Yvonne had a sinking feeling that she knew exactly who had done this, and his name was Edward Marvel Williams.

She went into her home office and turned on the computer. The first site she visited was YouTube, where she typed in the search terms "Tia and Robbie's wedding." The video popped right up. It had already received almost a million views. As Yvonne watched the entire fiasco for the second time, her heart went out to Tia, who was bound to be more mortified than ever before. And to think that she hadn't wanted to have her wedding at the church because she feared that people would talk about the fact that she was pregnant and unwed. *Well, they won't have time to talk about the pregnancy now,* Yvonne thought. *They'll all be too busy laughing at the fall-down drunk of a groom.*

As Yvonne watched Robbie try to stand up twice and then finally pass out, she saw something that had escaped her notice while the scene had played out in real time. She pressed the play button once more and watched it again, this time paying close attention to Robbie's eyes. They weren't red or bloodshot, as usually happened to someone when he'd had too much to drink. No, he didn't look drunk; he looked like he'd been drugged.

"Well, I'll be!" Yvonne said aloud as she marveled at how quickly she had come to side with the man who'd caused her daughter immense pain and humiliation. Okay, maybe she wasn't on his side exactly, but she at least believed his story. "Why'd you have to take the beer from Marvel in the first place, Robbie?" she wondered aloud.

She navigated from YouTube to her Google homepage, where she typed in the search terms "Yvonne Milner" + "Thomas Reed." Countless pages of results came up, many of them having to do with various conferences where both of them had preached. So, Yvonne started looking for the most recent items. When she found one with the word "pictures" in the heading, she clicked on the link. There she was in full color. In one photo, she was holding Thomas's hand, and in another, she was leaning against his shoulder. Both very innocent and easy to explain. But the other photos were not going to be so easily explained.

She and Thomas were staring into each other's eyes, then embracing. As Yvonne looked at those pictures, she recalled that very intimate moment—the moment that she and Thomas realized they could no longer pretend, and they leaned in closer and let their lips touch. The next photos showed just how passionate the kiss became. Yvonne closed her laptop without turning it off. She couldn't look at any more photos. Because those photos made something that had been a beautiful moment in time for her seem dirty and cheap.

She heard her front door open and figured that it was Toya. That, or one of those reporters had just broken into her house. The only other people who had keys to her home were Tia and Toya, and Tia was headed back to Chicago right now to pack up her things and move home. "Toya?" she called out.

"Yeah, Mama, it's me," her daughter shouted from downstairs.

Yvonne left her office and joined Toya in the living room.

"What's going on out there?" Toya demanded. "The moment I pulled up, those reporters bum-rushed me. They're saying that you and Uncle Thomas have been having an affair. Is that true, Mama?"

Never in a million years had Yvonne expected that she would ever need to explain her conduct to her children. And she really didn't want to start now. "What are you doing here? I thought you were going home to rest!"

"Marvel has a dinner party that he wants me to attend with him. So, I came over here to borrow one of your little black dresses."

"No, Toya, you can't go anywhere with that man. He's trying to destroy our family."

Toya backed up and lifted her hands to halt her mother. "Whoa, what are you talking about?"

"Marvel is out to get us. I don't know why, but you've got to trust me on this. That man taped Robbie's drunken behavior at the wedding and then posted the video on YouTube. And then he took pictures of me and Thomas...." She looked away, unable to finish her statement.

"So, it's true, then? You and Uncle Thomas were caught...k-i-s-s-i-n-g?" When she'd finished spelling the word with no protest from Yvonne, she put her hand over her mouth and stared in amazement. Her look wasn't accusatory, though. In fact, Yvonne thought she detected a bit of laughter in her eyes as she continued, "Mama, do I need to have the talk with you about boys and not letting them get to first base?"

"Hush up, Toya. This is not funny."

"Really, Mama, I don't see what the big deal is. If you and Uncle Thomas have feelings for each other, then I say go for it!"

"It's not that simple, Toya."

"Why isn't it? Daddy has been gone for almost two years, and Ms. Brenda has been dead longer than that, so there is nothing holding you back from being with each other. Just go for it, and quit being so secretive about everything."

"I'm not being secretive, and Thomas and I have not been sneaking around. The kiss just happened—that's it, and that's all. But you and I need to talk about Marvel. I want you to stay away from him, Toya."

Shaking her head, Toya said, "I really like Marvel, Mama. He's the first guy I've been totally into in a long time. And I don't think he's responsible for any of the things you're trying to pin on him. He told me you were paranoid, and I'm starting to believe him."

With her hands on her hips, Yvonne said, "Even if I am paranoid, Toya, it doesn't mean that Marvel isn't really out to get me."

Toya threw up her hands. "This is too much for me. I'm leaving. You can keep your black dress. I'll just go buy myself a new one."

"Don't leave yet, Toya. We still need to discuss this."

"There's nothing to discuss, Mama. I'm not trying to interfere with your relationship with Uncle Thomas, and I don't want you trying to interfere with my relationship with Marvel. Good night." Toya opened the front door and quickly closed it behind her.

Yvonne wanted to run after her daughter. She needed to chase the boogeyman away from her. But when she looked out the window, she saw that a handful of reporters were still staking out her home. She lifted her eyes to heaven. "Lord, I need You to open Toya's eyes," she prayed.

The phone rang. Yvonne was tempted not to answer it, but then she looked at the caller ID and saw that it was Thomas. "Thomas, we're in trouble," she said when she picked up the phone.

"Were reporters waiting on you when you got home, too?" he asked.

"Yes. And one just called me. They have a video of the wedding, plus pictures of us in a very intimate moment. I just reviewed all of the sordid mess online, and I'm just about sick to my stomach."

"I know. Vonnie, I'm so sorry. I never should have kissed you like that, but I couldn't help myself. For weeks now, I have tried to banish the feelings I have for you, but they just won't go away."

"Why would someone do this to us, Thomas? I mean, what's the point? We're two consenting adults! And poor Robbie. I just watched that video, and I have to tell you that I actually believe him about not being drunk. I got a good look at his eyes in that video, and he looked like he'd been drugged."

"I think the whole point is to discredit us in the eyes of the city council members, so that when we go before them about this land issue, we are so tarnished that no one cares what we want done about anything."

"So, you think Marvel did this to us, too?" Yvonne asked, excited that she could finally express her thoughts. She hadn't mentioned her suspicion of Marvel to Thomas, because Toya was right about one thing—she had been accusing that man of just about everything lately, and she hadn't wanted Thomas to think she was paranoid, too.

"Marvel has something to do with this. I'm almost sure of it."

"I wish you could tell that to Toya. She just left here in a huff because I accused her boyfriend of trying to destroy our family. She had the nerve to say that I was just paranoid, and I wanted to knock some sense into that girl's head. But you know as well as I do that the heart sees only what it wants to see."

"We're just going to have to come up with some proof to convince her that this guy is a snake."

A beep indicated that Yvonne had a call on the other line, but she ignored it. *Probably just another annoying reporter trying to get a so-called exclusive*, she thought. "What kind of proof can we find? I don't understand why he's bringing my daughter into this, either."

"There's a lot I don't understand, too. Where did this young man come from, and why does he have his sights set on the land occupied by our church? Like I said before, maybe we need to have the land evaluated to see if we're sitting on oil or something."

"If he's willing to do all of this to get it, a person would certainly think the land must be worth more than we know," Yvonne agreed.

"But you know what this tells me?" Thomas asked.

"What?"

"We must have made some headway with that guy at the mayor's office. I thought he wasn't interested in anything we had to say. But if Marvel felt he had to do this, then he must think it's a possibility that he could lose his bid on our property."

"What are we going to tell the congregation, Thomas? They are going to be mortified by all of this."

"We'll get through this, Vonnie. We've just got to trust that they will understand that we are two consenting adults who have fallen in love with each other."

Is that what they had done? No, wait a minute. Yvonne wanted to get off this ride and get back to the real world. She couldn't be in love with Thomas because she had promised to love David "always and forever." Those were the words she'd used just before he'd died. *Always and forever*. She couldn't just take those words back now, could she? "I've got to go, Thomas. I'll talk to you later."

They hung up, and as Yvonne sat back down, she realized that she was hyperventilating. She tried to calm her nerves by sheer will, which didn't work. Then, she remembered Ecclesiastes 5:5–6: *"Better not to vow than to vow and not pay. Do not let your mouth cause your flesh to sin, nor say before the messenger of God that it was an error. Why should God be angry at your excuse and destroy the work of your hands?"*

That was it. She had failed to keep her vow to her deceased husband, and now the works of her hands were being destroyed. The church building she and her husband had labored over would soon be torn down so that a factory could be erected in its place. Souls would be lost if Marvel got his way. And all because she hadn't been strong enough to keep her vow.

"My mom thinks you took those pictures of her and Uncle Thomas and that you videotaped my sister's drunken ex-fiancé," Toya told Marvel on their way to the dinner party at the mayor's. They were riding in Marvel's BMW.

"Your mom is completely paranoid. Why would I do something like that to my girlfriend's family?"

"I don't know, Marvel. You tell me. Why would you do something like that?"

"Listen to you! Don't tell me that you believe what your mom is saying about me. She doesn't like me, Toya, so naturally she is going to blame me for anything bad that happens."

Toya remembered that Marvel's car had been stolen a few weeks ago, and yet Marvel had never said a word about the police having found it. "When did you get your car back?"

"Last week. Did I forget to tell you? Anyway, I can tell you about that later. I was just thinking that maybe I should start attending church with you."

Toya gave him a look like he had lost his mind. "Marvel, I seriously doubt that you should be attending

my mom's church when she thinks you're trying to destroy our family—and the church building."

"You know what they say," Marvel quipped. "Keep
your friends close and your enemies closer."

Chapter
Sixteen

*Y*VONNE WAS HAVING A BAD DAY. AS IF THAT WAS something unusual. If she'd thought her church members had been dissatisfied with her behavior before, that was nothing compared to the way they felt now. Several members had informed her to her face that if she didn't stop carrying on with Thomas Reed, they would leave Christ-Life and join a "respectable" church immediately.

What upset the members of Christ-Life the most was the fact that the tabloids were claiming that Yvonne and Thomas had started their affair while David was lying on his sickbed and now felt free to rekindle their love because he was dead. Thomas dismissed the entire thing as silly and figured it would blow over quickly. But Yvonne valued her good name and had never had her character or motives questioned as they were being now. And it hurt.

Even though she knew that she wasn't guilty of what she was being accused of having done to her beloved husband, she felt ashamed. Yvonne had loved David until the day he died, and she loved him still. How people could be cruel enough to say the awful things they were saying about her, Yvonne simply didn't know.

But she also didn't have time to ponder the issue. Yvonne stood up and put on her white pastor's robe. She had a sermon to preach, and Thomas had a baptism to perform. As she walked out of her office and headed down the hallway toward the sanctuary, Thomas met up with her.

"Are you okay?" he asked, stepping alongside her.

"Yeah, sure," she said without looking at him.

"You've just been a little distant lately, so I wanted to make sure that I hadn't done anything to upset you."

"Thomas, this is not the place to discuss this. The gossips already have a mouthful of things to say about us. Let's not give them anything more. Okay?"

"Okay, Vonnie. We'll talk about this later."

"That's another thing," Yvonne said. "Call me Yvonne. If people hear you calling me Vonnie, they'll think all sorts of things."

Thomas grabbed her arm, halting her. "I don't care what these people say, *Yvonne*. I care about you, and I'm not going to let wagging tongues make me feel bad about it."

Yvonne pulled her arm out of his grip and walked into the sanctuary. How was she supposed to preach with Thomas on her mind? But it turned out that she didn't have to preach at all. The congregation went wild during Mike's baptism. The people began to shout, the choir sang three extra songs, and then Thomas continued to baptize people.

It started with Robbie rushing down the aisle and begging Thomas to baptize him, too, after Mike's baptism was complete. Many of the congregants probably recognized him as the guy who'd made a fool of himself in the YouTube video, so when he stood at the altar with bowed head and repentant heart, they got excited and started praising the Lord. Yvonne didn't know what made Robbie come to the altar, but she sure wasn't going to question it. She was smart enough to know a move of God when she saw one.

Thomas came down from the pulpit area and stood face-to-face with Robbie. "Do you remember when I told Mike that baptism doesn't mean anything without salvation?"

"I remember," Robbie said.

"So, did you come down to this altar to give your life to Christ?" Thomas asked him.

Tears formed in Robbie's eyes as he confessed, "I can't do this on my own. I need God's help. So, yes, I came down here to give my life to Christ."

"All right, then. Raise your hands and repeat after me...."

Robbie lifted his hands and repeated, "Lord God, I know that I am a sinner, but I believe that Jesus Christ is Your Son, and that He died to set me free from sin...."

After the service, Robbie asked if he could speak with Tia and Yvonne in her office. Yvonne agreed. She escorted them into her office, then sat down behind her desk, inviting Robbie and Tia to sit on the couch. Robbie turned to Tia and said, "First, I want to apologize to you. You were right when you said that I wasn't taking responsibility for my own actions. I shouldn't have drunk that beer."

"But you did, Robbie, and now we are the laughingstock of every person with a computer. Do you know how embarrassing it is that so many people have witnessed the nightmare you put me through?"

Robbie stood up and paced the floor. Then, he stopped and turned to Yvonne. "Do you remember when Pastor Reed was talking to me and Mike about giving our lives to Christ, but I wasn't interested?"

Yvonne nodded. "I remember."

He ran his hand through his short Afro. "Well, this week has been the worst week of my life. That video was plastered all over the Internet, and then my brother didn't want to drink with me."

A loud gasp escaped Tia's lips. "After everything that's happened, you still want to drink?"

He turned to Tia, pleading his case. "I didn't want to, but I didn't know how to stop myself, either. I was really messed up last week. You wouldn't talk to me. People kept calling and laughing at me because of that video. So, I went and purchased some beer and some real hard liquor. I took it over to Mike's place on Tuesday night, but he refused to even let me in the door. I went back to his house on Wednesday night and Thursday night, and he told me that I was being used by the devil to tempt him.

"When I woke up Friday morning, I finally admitted that I had a problem. I found out about an Alcoholics Anonymous meeting, so I went in there and spilled my guts. I thought I would feel better about myself and stop drinking like Mike did. But I had a beer right after I left the meeting."

Tia got up from the couch, rolling her eyes and flapping her hands in the air as she walked to the door. "I'm done with you."

Robbie grabbed her arm and said, "No, wait! Let me finish."

When it appeared that Tia was going to walk out the door anyway, Yvonne said, "Tia, the least you can do is hear him out."

Rolling her eyes again, Tia returned to her seat on the couch.

Robbie followed her, sat down next to her, and took her hand in his. "When I came to church today and watched Mike go down in that water and then come up looking so free, I realized right then that although I hadn't been able to admit it when we were in the Bahamas, I need Jesus. And when I went to the altar to give my life to Him, it felt like I was leaving my troubles behind, like the past no longer mattered. And you know what, Tia?"

"What, Robbie?"

"I still feel that way. What I did to you was awful. But it's in the past. All I can do is apologize and hope that you are ready to move forward with me and our baby."

"What do you mean by 'move forward'?" Tia asked.

"I want you to marry me, of course. I want us to be a family."

Tia held up a hand. "Just hold up one minute. Now, this whole speech you just made about giving your life to Christ was wonderful, but I still don't know if I can trust you with my life—or our baby's life."

Yvonne was so proud of her baby girl. Tia was stronger than she had ever given her credit for being. Thomas had seen the growth in Tia, but somehow, she—her own mother—had missed it. From this day forward, she wouldn't underestimate her child again.

"Don't you get it, Tia? I want to marry you and take care of you and our baby."

"Look, Robbie. From what I see, you can't even take care of yourself. So, you work on taking care of yourself, and then you can come talk to me about what you want to do for me and the baby."

"How are you going to take care of a baby by yourself, Tia? You don't even have a job!"

Tia stood up again. Her belly was protruding slightly underneath her form-fitting turquoise dress. Tia put her hand over her stomach as she said, "I dropped out of art school and moved back home with my mom this weekend. And I will be looking for a job starting tomorrow."

He stood next to her. "But what about us, Tia?"

"I don't know." She quickly turned and walked out of the room.

Robbie sank back into the couch and looked at Yvonne. "I've lost her, haven't I?"

Yvonne stood up and walked over to the couch. She sat down next to Robbie, filled with true compassion for the young man. She put her arm around his shoulder. "Tia still loves you, Robbie. You just need to give her some time to heal."

"But I've changed," Robbie declared with fire in his eyes. "I'm not the same man who did those terrible things to Tia. It's just like Pastor Reed said—Jesus set me free, and that means I'm free."

"I believe you, Robbie. All you have to do is stay on this path and lean on Jesus as you get your life in order. You've got to do it, Robbie, because my grandbaby is depending on you."

Tears filled Robbie's eyes again. "I know, and I promise you that I won't let him or Tia down ever again."

She gave Robbie a hug of encouragement. When they broke apart, there was a knock on the door, and Toya walked in with Thomas following behind. "I found lover boy out in the hallway lurking around, so I figured I'd bust into your office so he could have an excuse to see you," she said with a smirk on her face.

Toya must have thought she was quite amusing, but Yvonne did not find her comment funny in the least. "Toya, I really think that was an inappropriate thing to say," she told her with a scowl. "What if a church member heard you?"

"Mama, stop being a grouch. You've been crabby all week. What gives?" Toya complained as she closed the door.

Okay, maybe she had been in a bad mood all week. But that was only because she couldn't get Thomas out of her mind. One moment she wanted to be with him, and the next she felt guilty for thinking about him. The whole thing was maddening, and she didn't know what to do about it.

Robbie stood up. "I guess I'd better go."

Thomas walked over to Robbie and held out his hand. "I'm proud of you, young man. Keep walking with God."

Robbie shook Thomas's hand and grinned like a Grammy Award winner. "I will, sir. And thank you so much for what you've done for my brother and myself. Tia doesn't know it yet, but I'm a better man, and I owe it all to you."

"Give your thanks and praise to God, Robbie. It is the knowledge of Him that has made you better. Never forget that."

"I won't, sir," Robbie said as he turned to leave. Then, as he opened the door, he turned back to Thomas and asked, "Can I call you sometime...just to talk?"

"Anytime," Thomas assured him.

Smiling again, Robbie left the room.

"Now, do you two need a chaperone, or can I go?" Toya asked, looking from Thomas to Yvonne.

Yvonne picked up one of the pillows from the couch and threw it at her. "Get out of here, Toya, and don't come back until you can control that smart mouth of yours."

"Touché, touché," Toya said as she backed out of the room.

When the door closed behind her, Thomas shoved his hands in his pockets and gave Yvonne a sheepish smile. "She has a point, you know."

Yvonne stared at the floor. She refused to look at Thomas. He was her every weakness, and she wasn't going to crumble today. Not ever. "What are you talking about, Thomas?"

"You have been a grouch the past few days. Every time I try to talk to you, you either bark at me or ignore me like you're doing right now."

"I'm not ignoring you."

"You won't look at me, Yvonne. Don't you think I can tell that you've been avoiding me? Just tell me what I did that was so wrong, and I'll make it right. But talk to me, Vonnie—that's the only way we are going to get anywhere."

I don't want to get anywhere with you, she wanted to scream at him. But this really wasn't his fault. He had no idea that she had made a vow of forever love to a dead man, and that she planned to keep that vow until the day she joined David in the hereafter.

Thomas sat down next to Yvonne and lifted her chin with his hand. "Look at me, Vonnie. Tell me what's wrong."

She saw sadness in those beautiful hazel eyes of his, and she wanted to comfort him, but she was afraid that he would take any gesture of kindness the wrong way. So, she turned away from him again. "Nothing's wrong, Thomas. I just think that we need to keep our relationship on a professional level."

He jerked backward as if she'd just slapped him, then lowered his head and clasped his hands behind his neck. When he looked back up, he asked, "Is that what you want, Vonnie—for us to just be *professional* with each other?"

She heard the hurt in his every word. She closed her eyes for a moment and prayed for strength. When she opened them, Thomas was standing over her, waiting for a response. "Look, Thomas. Haven't we given the gossips and the news media enough to talk about? You are an international figure. You don't want this thing to spread any further than it already has."

His eyes flashed with anger. "I don't care what people say about us. I'm in love with you, Vonnie, and I thought that you felt something for me, too. Was I wrong?"

"I can't go there with you right now. Just leave it alone, okay?"

"No, I won't leave it alone. I need to know what you feel. Can you at least tell me that?"

"Okay, fine. You want to know how I feel?" She stood up from the couch and got in Thomas's face. "I think about you all the time. Does it make you feel better to know that? I hope it does, because it makes me feel guilty—guilty as sin every time I think about you when I promised my husband that I would love him forever."

Thomas calmed down, sighed, and gently touched her face. "You have nothing to feel guilty about. Our spouses are in heaven, but we are still very much alive."

"But I promised—"

"You kept all your promises to David while he was alive. You don't owe him your heart exclusively even after he's gone. I have made my peace with the fact that Brenda is never coming back. I think it's time you do the same."

"That's easy for you to say. You never cared one way or the other about Brenda, anyway."

He removed his hand from her face and stepped back with that wounded expression on his face again. "I cared very much for Brenda. She was my wife. We may not have seen eye to eye on everything, but I tried to make my marriage work."

"That's a crock. You never tried to make anything work; you just ran. You were away from home so much when Brenda was alive that I felt sorry for her."

"That's not fair, Yvonne—"

"Oh, so I'm 'Yvonne' rather than 'Vonnie' when I'm telling you the truth about yourself?" she interrupted him, hands on her hips. She was spitting venom at him, and she wanted to stop, but it was her only defense against the temptation he caused her.

"When David was alive, you traveled all over the country, speaking at this conference and that revival. How dare you accuse me of neglecting my family when you did the same!"

She held up a hand, giving him the five-finger disconnect. "Look, David. I don't want to have this discussion right now."

His eyes flashed angrily. "My name is Thomas," he said evenly, then turned and walked out of her office without another word.

Yvonne folded her arms around her waist and hugged herself as a tear rolled down her face. "I know your name," she whispered.

Chapter Seventeen

ON MONDAY, THOMAS WENT TO FLINT TO HAVE LUNCH with Jarrod. They were seated at Outback Steakhouse, eating their Bloomin' Onion appetizer, while waiting on the steaks and baked potatoes they'd ordered.

"So, what's with the sour mood, Dad?"

"I'm not in a sour mood," Thomas said as he tore into the Bloomin' Onion like it owed him money or something.

"If you say so."

Thomas wanted to talk about anything but his troubles. He looked at his son and asked, "How are things going with you and Missy?"

"Her name is Marissa, and that ended two weeks ago."

Their server came to the table and set a steak platter in front of each of them. They thanked her, and as she walked away, Thomas asked, "What happened?"

"Let's just say that she had way too many issues for me. And you were right. She couldn't cook a lick." Jarrod laughed after saying that.

"Just be glad you found out before you got too involved, son. Some women can suck you in by acting all sweet, and then, once they know they have you right where they want you, they flip the switch and bring out their real personality."

Jarrod put down his fork. "What happened between you and Auntie Yvonne?"

"What makes you think something happened?"

"Because the day I called about the kissing scene between the two of you, all you said was, 'It was bound to come out'—like it didn't bother you at all that your business was all over the Internet and in the gossip sections of the local papers."

"It wasn't as if that didn't bother me, but those pictures had captured the truth. I did kiss Yvonne. So, what else could I do but accept the fact that everyone knew and move on with life?"

"That's exactly what I'm talking about. You weren't disgruntled when you had a right to be. But now you're in such a sour mood that if you weren't a man of faith, I'd put you on a suicide watch."

"Whatever, Jarrod. I'm not that bad."

"Are you going to tell me what happened or not?"

Thomas had been pushing his food around on his plate, trying to avoid eye contact with his son. But then he came to the realization that he wasn't fooling anyone, especially not Jarrod. So, he put his fork down and looked his son in the eye. "Yvonne feels guilty about having feelings for me." Rolling his eyes heavenward, he continued, "I guess she thinks that since David died, she is never supposed to be happy another day in her life."

"Did Auntie Yvonne really say that?"

"Basically. She told me that she promised to love David forever, and that she can't just go back on her vow because of me."

"Wow. I guess I would have been upset if you had found another woman a few months after Mom died. But it's been two years! And it's been almost that long for Auntie Yvonne, too."

"That's what I told her, but then she began criticizing me, saying things I don't even want to repeat. I couldn't believe that she'd cut me down like that. But let's talk about something else. Okay?"

"Hey, handsome number one and handsome number two!"

At the familiar voice, both Thomas and Jarrod looked up to see Toya standing at their table with a wide grin on her face. Since childhood, Toya had called Jarrod "handsome." They had this cat-and-mouse game they always played with each other. Thomas stood up and hugged her. "Hey, Toya! What brings you to Flint?"

"Oh no, Daddy," Jarrod interjected. "Before you ask her any questions, she has to answer one for me first." He also stood up and hugged Toya, then pulled out a chair for her to sit in.

"What's your question, Bubba?"

That was Toya's other name for Jarrod, Thomas remembered.

"Which one of us is handsome number one, and which one is number two?" Jarrod asked.

"Oh, you are so conceited. It's no wonder you're not married yet. You probably can't find a woman to put up with you."

Jarrod put his elbows on the table and leaned closer to Toya. "Maybe I just haven't dated the right woman."

"Sorry, but this beautiful woman is already taken." Thomas looked up as Marvel came and stood behind Toya, who stood up and took Marvel's hand.

Jarrod shook his head. "I guess I missed out again, huh, Toya?"

"Whatever, Bubba. You were never serious about me, always too busy being a playboy."

Thomas picked up his napkin and wiped his mouth. "Toya, you never did tell me what brought you to Flint."

"Marvel's giving me a tour of one of his factories. He wants me to draw up some contracts for him."

Thomas eyed Marvel warily. "Well, you be careful, and call me if you need me."

Jarrod took that opportunity to take a business card out of his wallet and hand it to Toya. "You can call me, too. No sense in being a stranger when we're practically family."

Toya laughed. "Boy, you better behave." She took the card from Jarrod's hand as she said, "But I will take your card, because if my mom and your dad get their act together, we may just need to plan a wedding for them."

Thomas didn't say anything. He merely watched as Marvel put a protective hand on Toya's back and guided her away from the table. Since Toya's dad was gone, Thomas felt responsible for her and Tia. And right now, he wanted to rescue Toya from Marvel. But Toya was a grown woman, so he couldn't simply demand that she stop seeing this man. No matter how wicked Thomas thought Marvel was, Toya would have to see that truth for herself.

"Who's the guy?" Jarrod asked.

"Someone who is all wrong for Toya," Thomas muttered. "He's actually the same man who is trying to get the mayor to take the land the church sits on away from us."

"And Toya's *dating* him?" Jarrod asked.

"She doesn't think that Marvel is responsible. But I'll tell you something else: I believe he also took those pictures of me and Yvonne."

"You want me to go over there and rough him up?" Jarrod asked. "'Cause I'll do it if you want me to."

Thomas had no doubt that Jarrod could take Marvel in a fair fight. Jarrod was the same height as Thomas, and if he had stood up a few moments ago, he would have towered over Marvel. But Thomas knew from experience that Marvel didn't fight fair. "Trust me, you don't want to be anywhere near a fight with that man. He doesn't operate with the same moral code that we do." Then Thomas grinned and added, "Anyway, you just want to fight him because he's dating Toya. You had your chance with her when you two were teenagers, and you blew it. So leave her alone."

Jarrod groaned. "How many times do I have to tell you that I had no idea Toya wanted me to take her to the prom? If I had known, I wouldn't have taken that girl whose name I can't even remember now. But the past is the past, and Toya has grown to be a very beautiful woman."

"Yes, she has. She reminds me a lot of her mother. But as I said before, I don't want to talk about Yvonne."

"Look, Dad. If Auntie Yvonne really wants to be left alone, you're going to have a hard time complying if the two of you are working together."

"You're right about that. But I can't abandon her at a time like this just because she's making my life difficult."

"I'm not suggesting that you abandon her. But how about going on a road trip with me?"

"What kind of road trip?"

"Business, of course. I have a few accounts to check on. I'll probably be gone about a week, maybe two."

Thomas recalled how Yvonne had accused him of running away from Brenda when things had gotten tough for them. If he took this trip with Jarrod, she would surely think he was running away from her, too. But maybe they needed to spend some time apart.

She was so worried about what other people thought and said. If he wasn't around for a short period of time, perhaps the gossip would cool down, and she would be more receptive to him again.

"That sounds like a good idea," he finally said. "I would love to travel with you, son. If I can get back to Detroit before the city council meeting, it shouldn't be a problem."

"I'm going to be the one working, Dad, not you, so you can leave anytime you need to."

"All right, then. I'm going on a road trip with my son! I have a meeting with the governor of Michigan in the morning, but I'm free after that," Thomas told Jarrod.

They finished their meal, and when they parted ways, they agreed that Thomas would drive to Jarrod's house tomorrow, where their road trip would begin.

On the drive back to Detroit, Thomas kept thinking about the accusations that Yvonne had hurled at him. Her words had told him loud and clear what she thought of him. She believed that he always ran away when things got too hard. And if his previous track record was any indicator, he could see why. After all, he had given up on pastoring his church when it became clear that it could not succeed. Thomas had always felt that God had something else in mind for him, but he'd taken the pastoring route because everyone had expected it of him once he'd finished seminary. So, instead of pursuing the dreams that God had placed in his heart, he had done what seemed natural.

But what seemed natural for most seminary graduates had been like bondage to him because his heart had been out there—and "there" meant "everywhere." Thomas had had no clue how to go about traveling the world and delivering God's message while doing it, but while his church had been failing, his trust in God had grown. So, he'd hit the road, visiting churches and making a name for himself. In his eyes, he hadn't been running away from his responsibilities—he'd been running to them.

Thinking back on his early days as a traveling minister/motivational speaker, Thomas now realized that he had never really tried to make Brenda comfortable with his new role. He'd simply come home and informed her that he was going to take his ministry on the road. Brenda had cried and pleaded with him not to leave her alone, but Thomas's position had been that if Brenda didn't want to be alone, then she should travel with him. Oh, he'd known that she wouldn't be able to travel while Jarrod was in school, but during the summer months, he'd thought, the three of them could see the world together.

But Brenda had been comfortable at home and hadn't wanted to go anywhere. And then she'd tried to make him feel guilty because he wanted to be every-where but at home. He'd loved his wife—God knew he had. But the truth was, they were never truly suited for each other. Brenda would have had a much hap-pier life if she had married a man more like herself. When she died, Thomas had promised himself that he would never put another woman through the same heartache.

Thomas had just agreed to take a trip with his son, and he needed to make sure that Yvonne knew he wasn't running. He would take this trip to allow things to cool off between them, but he would be back.

As he drove down Interstate 75, he thought about what needed to be done before he left. He would drive to Detroit, pack a bag, then drive to Lansing for his morning meeting with the governor. Then, he'd head back to Flint so he could get on the road with his son. But before doing any of that, he needed to talk to Yvonne.

He picked up his cell phone and dialed her number. The phone rang several times, but she didn't pick up. Thomas wasn't sure if she was avoiding his call or if she simply was not near her phone. He was half tempted to hang up before the beep signaling that a voice mail was being recorded. But then, he decided that he had nothing to lose, so he would speak his mind and let her deal with it. "Hey, Vonnie," he began in a gentle tone that belied his memory of the knock-down, drag-out argument they'd had just yesterday. "I'm in my car, headed back home from Flint. Anyway, I wanted you to know that Jarrod asked me to go out of town with him for a few days, and I told him I would. But I'll be back before we have to meet with City Council."

He wanted to prevent Yvonne from thinking he was running away from their problems as soon as she heard that he was leaving, just as she thought he always did. So, he quickly added, "Did you hear me? I'll be back, Vonnie. I'm not running, just giving you the break that you seem to need."

He hung up, and even though he hadn't packed his bags yet, he missed Yvonne already. He prayed that she would get over this ridiculous notion about keeping a vow to a dead man and then learn to live and love again—with him.

Chapter Eighteen

THE PHONE RANG THREE TIMES BEFORE YVONNE EVEN looked at the caller ID. Then, she froze. It was Thomas. She felt so bad about the way she'd spoken to him earlier and really wanted to apologize. But she couldn't talk to him right now. She feared that if she spoke to him, she might just break her vow and declare her love for him. Now she was sorry that she'd ever agreed to let him stay and help her pastor the church.

Several minutes later, slumped in her couch, she listened helplessly to his message. He didn't sound angry, even though he had every right to be. She had had no business saying anything negative about his relationship with Brenda. If Thomas had wanted to chase the moon and the stars rather than be at home with his family, that was his business and none of hers.

According to his voice-mail message, he had just left Flint, so he was probably in a good mood after seeing Jarrod. But Yvonne's heart sank when she heard him say that he would be leaving town with his son.

A moment ago, she'd thought she was sorry for agreeing to let him stay, but now that he was leaving, it hurt to know that she would not see him every day, as she had for the past several months. Two tears escaped her watery eyes and rolled down her face. She would have to let him go. It was for the best. She just wasn't sure that her heart could bear another good-bye.

Just as she was about to fall apart, she heard Thomas say, "I'll be back, Vonnie. I'm not running, just giving you the break that you seem to need." And even though she didn't want to, she clung to his words. Because she knew with all of her being that if Thomas said he would be back, then he would.

She replayed his message because she wanted to hear his soft, baritone voice again.

About halfway through the message, Tia walked into the room and caught her drooling over Thomas's message. Yvonne slammed her cell phone shut, turned away, and grabbed the tissue box.

"Have you been crying?" Tia asked.

Yvonne wiped her face and then turned back around. "I was just having a moment. Nothing to worry about."

"Are you and Uncle Thomas fighting?" Tia asked as she plopped onto the couch, crossed her legs, and pulled her feet up under them.

"Why would you think that?"

"Because you look really sad, Mama. I remember from when I was a kid and you would get sad like this. It was always after some fight with Daddy about whether or not you were called to the ministry."

"Well, your father didn't believe that women should preach. And let me tell you, that man infuriated me so much in those days that I wanted to scream. I guess I often did."

Tia laughed. "Yeah, I don't know how many times Toya and I heard you tell Daddy that he needed to step into the twentieth century and get away from all his backward thinking. Toya would say, 'She told *him*.' And then we would hear Daddy say, 'Backward or not,

Yvonne Milner, I am your husband, and I say that you are not preaching anywhere.' And then I would turn to Toya and say, 'He told *her*.'"

Yvonne gave Tia a playful pinch. "You were always a big old daddy's girl. How come you couldn't have been on my side about that?"

Tia giggled and pulled away from her. "I'm on your side now, Mama, so stop the pinching. You know I hate that."

Yvonne stopped pinching Tia as she asked, "But why weren't you on my side back then? You didn't believe that women should preach when you were a child?"

"It didn't have anything to do with that, Mama. You've got to see this through the eyes of a child. You would get so sad after one of those arguments with Daddy that Toya would get mad and say that Daddy was unfair. So, I felt like someone needed to be on Daddy's side."

"And whose side do you think your baby is going to be on in the fight between you and Robbie?"

Tia looked away for a moment. When she turned back to Yvonne, her eyes were bubbling over with fresh tears. "I know I've made a mess of my life. If I had just listened to you, none of this would be happening right now. But I thought I knew better than God, and now I'm paying for my disobedience."

"Oh, Tia." Yvonne hugged her daughter tight. "I didn't mean to make you cry. There is entirely too much crying in this house. Remember what Paul wrote in Romans about all things working together for good for those who love God? Well, you love the Lord, and even though you made a mistake, your baby will be the blessing that He brings out of your repentance." When they pulled apart, Yvonne said, "And you do know that God can help you through single parenting, if that's what you choose to do, right?"

Nodding, Tia said, "I know that, Mama. That's why I'm not rushing to accept Robbie's proposal this time. I still love him; I'm not going to deny that. But if he really wants us to be a family, then he has to grow up."

"Are you hungry?" Yvonne asked.

"Starving."

"Good. Let's continue this conversation in the kitchen. I took some chicken breasts out of the freezer last night. We can grill them and make a salad."

Tia got up and followed Yvonne into the kitchen. "Okay, I'll eat the rabbit food, but I need some ice cream when we're done eating healthy. I want a whole bucket of cherries jubilee, or maybe Oreo. Better yet, I'll take some double chocolate chip mixed with cherries."

"Oh, goodness. I have four more months to deal with you and your cravings? Heaven help me," Yvonne teased.

Putting her hand over her belly, Tia said, "Hey, what baby wants, baby gets."

"Okay. We'll go out for ice cream after dinner, but only because my grandbaby wants it," Yvonne conceded.

Tia stuck out her tongue.

Yvonne laughed as she opened the refrigerator door and began to bring out various salad toppings, which Tia arranged on the counter. Then, after heating the grill, Yvonne seasoned the chicken breasts and put them on a platter to take outside.

"If it's any encouragement to you, Tia, I do think Robbie is sincere about giving his life to God," Yvonne said as she washed her hands.

"I hope he is, Mama. But I'm not trusting anything he says until I see that he has stopped drinking and can keep a job."

Yvonne dried her hands on a towel, then came to stand at the counter where Tia was slicing cucumbers and tomatoes. "I've been thinking about something," Yvonne said, leaning forward and propping her elbows on the counter.

"What's up?"

"Well, my publisher wants me to write another book. The idea appeals to me because I need something to do, something to take my mind off of things."

"Things? Like a tall, handsome preacher whose voice alone put tears in your eyes today?"

"Tia!" Yvonne admonished her.

Tia shrugged. "I'm just sayin', Mama. Toya and I both see it. Good grief, anyone with a computer can see that you and Uncle Thomas have a thing for each other, with the way he was kissing you and all."

"With you being the big daddy's girl that you are, I don't understand why you aren't upset with me."

"I probably would be if things hadn't gone so wrong with me and Robbie. Having to go through that made me realize that you can't help who you love. And it also helped me to understand that you have every right to have someone special in your life."

Yvonne was speechless. She hadn't expected Tia to be so calm and rational about this. But Tia seemed to be handling it better than she was. When Yvonne was finally able to speak again, all she could say was, "Can we get back to what I was talking about?"

Tia continued chopping the vegetables. "Sorry for interrupting. Go right ahead—don't face reality."

Yvonne cleared her throat. "As I was saying, my publisher wants me to write a book, and I was wondering if you might like to work on this book with me."

Tia's eyes grew wide, the way they did whenever something took her by surprise. "What?"

"You heard me."

"You actually want me to work on your book with you? What would it be about?"

"I think we should write it for young adults, make it something that will help guide them through this tough age...and help them understand why it's always better to follow God, even if the rest of the world is doing its own thing. What do you think?"

"Well, I certainly think I have something to say on that subject. I definitely don't want anyone else to end up in the same position that I'm in. So, yes, I'm in!" Tia put down the knife and gave her a hug. "Thanks, Mama! I've always wanted to write a book. I just never had anything to say before."

"You certainly do now, Tia. You really have grown in so many ways through this experience. I believe that you are right in the place where God can finally use you."

Meanwhile, Toya was right in a place of indecision. Marvel had invited her over to his house for dinner and a movie. He'd cooked a fabulous chicken-shrimp scampi, and it had been so good that Toya had helped herself to seconds.

After dinner, Marvel had begun washing the dishes, and he'd refused Toya's offer to help. So, she'd asked if she could check her e-mail on his computer. He'd agreed, but he must have forgotten that his own e-mail account was still open. Now, she was staring at an e-mail from Clarence Brown, the former deacon and finance director at Christ-Life Sanctuary, who had run off with hundreds of thousands of dollars that belonged to the church.

Why would Deacon Brown be e-mailing Marvel? Toya wondered. In fact, she wanted to know so bad that she broke the cardinal rule of dating, "No snooping," by opening the message and reading it.

Marvel,

Don't think the piddling two thousand dollars you brought me today is going to shut me up. I am the one who helped you get what you needed from City Council. I took that money from my church and squandered it because you said you would pay me five times the amount of money I took, just as long as I made sure that Christ-Life couldn't pay its bills, so that you could convince the members of City Council that you should be allowed to take over that area. As if you were doing them a favor, saving them from having foreclosed property on their hands.

Just remember, I know everything about you, and I am more than willing to tell City Council—and the mayor himself—all about the undocumented work-ers you fill your factories with. So, don't play with me, Marvel. Send me my money so I can leave the coun-try, and you'll never hear from me again.

"Are you finished yet, babe?" Marvel called from the kitchen. "I'm ready to put the movie on."

"Almost," Toya responded. She thought that he might come into the office, so she quickly closed Dea-con Brown's e-mail message and shut down the com-puter. Her mind was racing as she tried to figure out what to do.

Marvel had said that he'd never told the mayor that he specifically wanted the property where her mother's church was located. But Deacon Brown's e-mail indicated that he had not only asked for that land but had also conspired with Deacon Brown to ensure that Christ-Life would be in no financial position to fight him off. Marvel was a snake, just like her mother had said.

Now she needed to figure out what she was going to do about this serpent she had allowed into the garden of her affections. Toya had thought that Marvel was for real—that he was interested in her for who she was and what she brought to the table. After all, she was a good catch. She was an attorney who made six figures and had the potential to make millions during her career. Besides that, she was a beautiful black woman who loved the Lord. As far as Toya was concerned, that meant far more than her earning potential. But Marvel couldn't see her true worth. He obviously just saw her as a pawn in his sick little game.

Toya had just closed his computer and was turning around when Marvel came to the door and leaned against the doorjamb. "Are you going to keep me waiting all night, babe? I thought we were supposed to leave business at the door and just enjoy each other."

She had been the one to suggest that they leave business at the door when Marvel's business had started interfering with her mother's church, which had made Toya feel like she was caught in the middle. She stood up and walked toward him, strutting in her Donna Karan pantsuit, which touched every curve of her body.

"Did I tell you how good you look tonight?" he asked, looking her up and down.

"No," she said as she stood before him, wishing that she had something heavy in her hand so that she could bash him over the head with it.

"Well, you do. You look so good, Toya, that I'm always proud to have you on my arm."

Toya thought it strange to see no guile in Marvel's eyes as he spoke those words to her. Did he really care for her? And, if so, why was he trying to destroy her mother's church? Toya had no clue how Marvel's mind worked, but she planned to find out. Not long ago, he had told her that he kept his friends close and his enemies even closer. Well, Toya planned to do the same. "Let's go watch that movie, Marvel."

"I don't know," Marvel said with hunger in his eyes. "Now that I'm this close to you, I think I'd rather be doing something else. Like kissing my lady." He bowed his head and brought his lips to meet hers.

She had enjoyed Marvel's kisses and had even gotten lost in them a time or two. But now that she knew him for the rotten snake he was, his kiss was foul to her. She needed to move away from him before she became ill. She knew she couldn't move too fast, though, or Marvel would suspect that she was upset with him.

When the kiss was over, she said again, "Let's go watch that movie."

Marvel sighed. "Always the good girl, huh, Toya?"

"Actually, Marvel, you have no clue just how bad I can be. But I think I'm going to show you one day real soon."

Chapter Nineteen

*Y*VONNE HAD NEVER SEEN TOYA AS ANGRY AS SHE WAS right now. Shortly after eleven that night, her older daughter had barged into the house and awakened her and Tia to tell them about Marvel's scheme and Deacon Brown's involvement in it. "I don't know why I didn't believe you in the first place, Mama," she said, slumping onto the living room couch next to Yvonne. "You have such keen intuition, and I am just the biggest fool who ever lived."

Tia leaned around Yvonne and raised her hand. "Sorry, sis. You might be the second biggest fool, but I've already claimed the title of biggest fool. And I have Robbie, Marvel, and YouTube to thank for that."

"Oh, Tia, I'm so sorry about that," Toya said, reaching across Yvonne's lap and patting Tia's leg. "I wish I had never even thought to invite Marvel to your wedding. He's such a creep. But I am going to make him pay for everything he has done to us. I promise you that."

Toya had a fire in her eyes that Yvonne had never seen before. "Calm down, sweetie," she interjected. "It's not your fault the guy you fell for had ulterior motives. I didn't raise any fools, so I don't want to hear either of you talking about being a fool again. Okay?"

"Well, what would you call it, Mama?" Tia asked. "I not only fell in love with an alcoholic—I got pregnant by him, too."

"That wasn't the wisest thing to do, true, but we're all prone to make mistakes, honey. That doesn't make you a fool."

Tia moved closer to Yvonne and leaned her head on her shoulder. "Well, then I feel like a fool, Mama, because the truth of the matter is, I still love Robbie, and even after all that he's done to me, I'm praying that becoming a Christian will help him to grow up so that we can be a family."

"And what about me?" Toya asked as she leaned her head against Yvonne's other shoulder. "Even though I know that Marvel is a low-down snake, I still think he's kind of cute."

Yvonne laughed. "Look, you two. Right now, I'm the last one who should be giving out relationship advice. I'm dealing with something that I'd never expected to be dealing with."

Toya sat up and looked Yvonne in the eyes. "Mama, don't be mad at me for saying this, but I think you need to give Uncle Thomas a chance. He looked so sad when I saw him earlier today."

"Where did you see Thomas?" Yvonne asked. She tried to sound nonchalant, but inside, her stomach was fluttering at the mere mention of his name.

"I went to Flint with Marvel today, and we ran into Uncle Thomas and Jarrod at Outback Steakhouse," Toya said, then gasped. "Oh my gosh! Marvel totally played me!"

"What do you mean?" Yvonne asked.

"Remember how I told you that Deacon Brown's e-mail indicated that Marvel had given him some money today? Well, I was with Marvel all day, and the only time he could have given Deacon Brown that money was while we were in Flint." Toya started pounding her fist against her head. "I'm so stupid, stupid, stupid."

"Toya!" Yvonne admonished her. "Your father and I spent too much money on your education for you to be stupid, thank you very much."

Toya stood up and started pacing the floor. "Marvel must have gotten some sort of sick pleasure out of having me with him while he paid off the man who stole money from our church."

"What are you talking about?" Tia asked.

"I know where Deacon Brown is," Toya announced with hands raised as if she were getting ready to do a praise dance.

"Did the e-mail say something about his location?" Yvonne asked.

"No, but Marvel took me right to him. See, I thought he was trying to impress me by taking me to his factory in Flint. But he must have dropped off the money for Deacon Brown at some point during the day. It probably gave him quite a thrill to know that I was right there with him, and that he pulled it off right under my nose."

Tia sat up and stretched. "Should we really be calling him Deacon Brown?" she asked her mother. "I'm sure you've excommunicated him by now. Can't we just call him 'Clarence' or 'Mr. Brown'?"

"I'd like to speak with the man before we just throw him out of the church," Yvonne replied. "Deacon Brown has been a respected member of Christ-Life for over twenty years. I don't know why he would do a thing like this, but I'd like to hear him out."

"Oh, we've already heard him out," Toya said, shaking her head. "I told you what his e-mail said. And now, I'm going to make sure that he gets arrested." She picked up her purse and searched around inside for a few moments before pulling out a small card. She turned it over, pulled out her cell phone, and dialed.

"Who are you calling?" Yvonne asked her.

"Jarrod. He gave me his number when I saw him today, and I'm about to put him to work."

Yvonne and Tia listened as Toya greeted Jarrod, apologized for waking him up at so late an hour, and then got right down to business. She told him about Marvel Williams and Clarence Brown and informed him that the former deacon was hiding out in a certain motel. She asked him to call the police and then meet them there.

When their conversation ended, she hung up and turned back to Yvonne and Tia. "Now we wait," she announced.

"How do you know that Deacon Brown is in that motel?" Yvonne asked. "Don't tell me you went there with Marvel today!"

"Mama, get real," Toya said, rolling her eyes. "I figured it out. Marvel stopped at this little hole-in-the-wall donut shop when we were on our way to grab lunch. I thought it was strange—why eat donuts when you're about to have a big steak-and-potatoes type of meal? So, I asked him why we were stopping. He told me that he really needed some coffee and that he would only be a minute. But when he came back out, he didn't have any coffee.

"When I asked him about it, he just blew it off and said that the donut shop didn't have any coffee ready. I didn't think much of it at the time, but when I mentioned to you that I'd seen Uncle Thomas and Jarrod in Flint, it reminded me of the strange stop Marvel and I made, and then I remembered that there was a motel right next to that donut shop. And I'd be willing to stake one week's pay on the fact that Clarence Brown is in that motel."

"We don't gamble in this house," Yvonne said in a mock-stern tone.

"You know what I mean. Let's just wait for Jarrod to call back, and then we'll see if I'm right or not."

Less than twenty minutes later, Jarrod called back, asking for a photo of Clarence Brown. Yvonne turned on her computer and e-mailed a photo of the deacon to Jarrod, who said he could access it on his phone.

Half an hour later, the house phone rang. Seeing that it was Thomas, Yvonne picked up. "Hey, Vonnie! Jarrod told me what's going on. The police have Clarence Brown in custody, and I'll be in Flint tomorrow to meet Jarrod. So, don't worry about a thing. I will talk to the man before I leave town."

"Thank you for taking care of this, Thomas," Yvonne said gratefully. "Oh, and I'm going to need that private investigator of yours for something else. Can you have him give me a call tomorrow at the church?"

"It's one o'clock in the morning, Vonnie, so it's already tomorrow. But I'll have him give you a call. And tell Toya I said she did good."

"I'll do that."

Yvonne hung up and told Toya, "Thomas is proud of you. He says you 'did good.'"

Smiling, Toya said, "And I'm not through. I've got some things planned that will make Mr. Marvel Williams's head spin."

Yvonne held up a hand. "I don't want you involved in this one second longer, Toya Ann Milner. Do you hear me?"

"But Mama, there's one more thing that e-mail mentioned that needs to be taken care of!"

"I know exactly where you're going with this, and that is why I told Thomas I need to speak with that private investigator. I will handle Mr. Marvel Williams, and you will stay far, far away from him. Do you understand me?"

"The city council meeting is in two weeks, Mama. We need to get some hard evidence against Marvel. We don't have any time to waste if you don't want to lose the church."

"You know what I've figured out through all of this madness, Toya?"

Toya sighed. "What?"

"I've found out that I can trust God. I prayed about the fact that you were deceived by that man, and God opened your eyes to the truth. So, I believe that if I handle the things I need to handle, God will also take care of the Marvels of this world. Trust your mama, sweetie. I've got a plan. Even better, God's got a plan."

The next day, Yvonne set her plan in motion. She wasn't about to do anything without prayer. So, she called all of her elders together and told them that she wanted to start a prayer vigil that would continue for the next two weeks. "I need you to get your committee members together and have them sign up church members to pray an hour at a time," she explained to the elders.

"An hour is a long time for some people to pray," one of the elders objected. "If we ask too much of the people, they might not do anything at all."

Yvonne was so tired of the hand-holding needed for members who just didn't understand what ministry was all about. *Do people really not comprehend that when you sign up to be a servant of the Lord, you just might get an uncomfortable assignment?* she wondered.

She thanked God for grace. If it wasn't for God's mercy, Yvonne honestly didn't know how some Christians would make it into heaven—herself included.

"Point taken," Yvonne said. "Let's first sign up all of our committee members, and then I'll put a call out for prayer among the congregation at large. We can ask them to pray for an hour but then slot them for only the first or the last half hour. That way, they won't feel obligated to pray for the entire hour. I'm still hoping that we'll get some prayer warriors who will go the distance, though."

Now that they had their marching orders, the elders began to file out of her office. Yvonne stopped Elder Conrad as he passed.

"How can I help you, Pastor?" he asked, taking a seat in front of her desk.

"If you have a moment, I'd like to know how the evangelistic team is handling their assignment."

"Everything is going well," Elder Conrad assured her. "We have divided up the list that Dawn gave us by geographical area, and team members have been making home visits for the past several weeks."

"And how are our former members doing? Are they mostly attending other churches, or do they stay home on Sunday mornings?"

"There's a mix. With the ones who indicated they had joined another church, we just thanked them for their time and informed them that the door of Christ-Life is always open, but as long as they are happy where they are, we aren't asking them to come back.

"With the former members who seemed to be struggling a bit and aren't attending a church at the moment, we've asked them to give us another try. Some of them just requested prayer, and we've been happy to pray with them. But a great number of the people we've seen so far have said that they will visit Christ-Life in the coming weeks."

"That's awesome. Thank you so much for your diligence on this, Elder."

By the time Elder Conrad left her office, Yvonne felt as if she was making progress. Many people had lost a sense of connection and had wandered away from the church because she had grieved so much that she hadn't noticed how her actions had been affecting the congregation. If it took her the rest of her life, Yvonne was determined to do right by the people whose spiritual care God had entrusted to her.

She opened her Bible and began to study God's Word. She had a sermon to preach on Sunday, and she aimed to make it her best one yet. She planned to preach about keeping the faith and moving past hurts and pains. She never liked to preach pie-in-the-sky messages about lessons she hadn't lived or proven in her own life. Yvonne was a firm believer that people go through tests and trials not based on where they are, but based on where they *say* they are. Many Christians claimed to have mountain-moving faith, but the truth was, many of them didn't believe that God would help them pay their bills if they didn't tithe on time.

Yvonne never wanted to claim to be somewhere that she wasn't. So, she was going to minister to her congregation out of her own hurts and pain. Then, she was going to tell them how she'd learned to trust God with her heart and life, even after losing her husband. She was going to tell them how she'd learned to live again.

There was a knock on her door.

Yvonne put her pen down and looked up. "Come in."

The door swung open and Dawn walked in, carrying a vase with a bouquet of about three dozen roses.

"I have something for you," she said with a knowing smile.

"For me?" Yvonne said, staring blankly. "Who would send me roses?"

"I don't know, but there is a card. You might just find your answer there." Dawn set the vase on the desk, handed Yvonne a small envelope, and backed out of the office, still wearing a big grin.

When the door was closed again, Yvonne opened the envelope and pulled out the card. It said, "I'm not running anymore, Vonnie. I'll see you soon and we'll work everything out." He hadn't signed the card, but he hadn't needed to.

Now what was she supposed to do about this?

Chapter Twenty

YVONNE HADN'T BEEN BUGGED BY A REPORTER SINCE Thomas had left town with Jarrod a little over a week ago. With all the snoops leaving her alone for a change, she'd managed to have a productive week. She had called a congregational meeting at which she had dispelled the rumors about Thomas and her alleged affair, and it seemed that most everyone understood that they had been set up. Then, she had even driven to Flint and talked to Clarence Brown herself. But the visit had been rather uneventful. She hadn't been able to get anything more out of the man than what Thomas had already told her.

What really bugged Yvonne about Clarence's silence is that she had been prepared to pardon him if he had just asked. But Clarence wasn't interested in a pardon. He held to the claim that he had done nothing wrong and had been arrested on fabricated charges. He'd even gone so far as to tell Yvonne that she should be ashamed of herself for running to the police and filing charges against him before she'd had a chance to hear his side of things.

"I wanted to hear your side, Clarence, but you skipped town and made it impossible for me to do anything else but believe that you were the one who stole the money," Yvonne had explained.

Clarence hadn't appeared fazed by what she'd had to say. He'd preferred to play the victim. "I had been at Christ-Life for more than twenty years, and I would have thought that since I served you and your husband faithfully and did whatever was asked of me, I would have been given the benefit of the doubt."

Yvonne had wanted to remind Clarence that he had just attempted to have her thrown out of her own church but thought better of going tit for tat with the man. Again, it had been obvious that Clarence wasn't seeking redemption right now, so she'd seen no reason to linger. Yvonne had left the prison and gone straight back to Detroit. There was so much to do, and she didn't have a minute to waste.

Sunday's service had been an awesome and humbling experience. Hundreds of former members had come back to church and bombarded the altar when she'd made the call for those who needed to receive salvation and rededicate their lives to the Lord to come forward. And the thing that had topped off her day was when she'd walked back to her office after the service to find her desk adorned with another vase filled with roses.

Thomas had called her every night since he'd left to talk about church business, the upcoming city council meeting, his travels with Jarrod, and the things that were going on with the girls. They hadn't gotten personal beyond the surface level, though, and had not even mentioned the issue that had been between them since the night Yvonne had blown up at Thomas.

After they talked on Friday night, Yvonne put on her bathrobe and a pair of house slippers and walked downstairs to get a snack, all the while wondering why Thomas hadn't brought up the issue of their relationship. He'd been sending roses, along with boxes of chocolates with adorable messages, on an almost daily basis. So, why not talk about it?

She selected a Granny Smith apple from the bowl on the counter and washed it, then opened the refrigerator and took out a block of Colby cheese. When she'd sliced both the fruit and the cheese on the cutting board, she arranged them on a plate, grabbed a napkin, turned off the kitchen light, and headed back upstairs. It was nice, in a way, to have the house to herself again. Tia was at a singles' outing organized by the church. So, with snack in hand, Yvonne closed her bedroom door and hoped to find a movie on the Hallmark Channel that she could watch until she fell asleep.

Her Fridays hadn't always been this humdrum, especially when David was alive. Often, they would go out to dinner and catch a movie. On the nights they stayed home, Yvonne and David still enjoyed their time together. But now that Yvonne thought about it, she had spent a lot of Friday nights on the road, traveling to one conference after the next. She'd thought that life would be so great once her name was as well-known as Joyce Meyer's. In reality, though, she'd missed many special moments with her husband and her children, and she regretted having chided Thomas for how much time he'd spent away from home. Although she might not have spent as much time away as he had, she still could have been home more.

Once David had finally accepted her call from God to preach, Yvonne had convinced herself that she needed to make up for lost time by scheduling as many speaking engagements as she could. In hindsight, she should have spent a little more time loving her family and a little less time chasing after the wind. For even though she had become well-known, she still wasn't a household name, and now she didn't even care.

Yvonne would gladly spend the rest of her days ministering to her own congregation and never accept another speaking engagement if only she had a husband to come home to. But how could she ever have that with David gone forever?

With the remote in one hand, Yvonne surfed through the TV channels, feeding herself slices of apple and pieces of cheese with the other. The Hallmark Channel was showing another Janette Oke movie, but Yvonne had already seen each of them about a hundred times, so she turned off the TV and grabbed her Bible from the side table. Somewhat haphazardly, she flipped the pages to the Song of Solomon and read, *"Let him kiss me with the kisses of his mouth; for your love is better than wine."*

Yvonne dropped her jaw and raised her eyebrows in shock. She knew what the Song of Solomon was about, but she hadn't read from the beginning for so long that she'd forgotten how the book started out. Why in the world would she read something like that when she didn't have a husband anymore? But even as she asked herself that ridiculous question, Yvonne knew that she wanted to read this particular book because of the way Thomas had kissed her. She hugged her Bible close to her heart as she whispered, "Oh, God, why did he have to kiss me?"

Yvonne knew of one thing that would take her mind off of Thomas: the memory of the vow she'd made to David. She turned to the fifth chapter of Ecclesiastes. Usually, whenever she read this chapter, she paid close attention to verses five and six: *"Better not to vow than to vow and not pay. Do not let your mouth cause your flesh to sin, nor say before the messenger of God that it was an error. Why should God be angry at your excuse and destroy the work of your hands?"* But to-night, verse four seemed to glare at her: *"When you make a vow to God, do not delay to pay it; for He has no pleasure in fools. Pay what you have vowed."*

For so long, Yvonne had been condemning herself with verses five and six, thinking that if she didn't honor her vow to David, then God had every right to destroy the works of her hands. But the fifth verse in Ecclesiastes wasn't talking about any vow made to man, for the verse preceding it said that a vow made to God must be kept. Not that Yvonne didn't think that the vows made to fellow human beings were impor-tant, but she was finally beginning to see that God did not expect her to uphold the promise she'd made to her husband on his deathbed to the point of closing her heart to love for the rest of her life.

Closing her Bible, Yvonne glanced at the bouquet of pink roses, Peruvian lilies, and butterfly asters in a vase on her dresser. Thomas had sent it yesterday—a "Happy Thursday" gift, he'd called it—and she'd found it so pretty that she hadn't been able to bear leaving it at work. Besides, she had so many flowers in her office right now that the place was beginning to look like a funeral home. She knew she should give some of the flowers away or throw them out, but she couldn't bring herself to do it. Good thing Thomas was due back in town in three days.

Yvonne put her hand over her mouth when she caught herself smiling at the thought of seeing Thomas in a few days. Okay, maybe she had realized that God was not asking her to keep a promise of exclusive love to her husband since he wasn't living anymore. But her heart still didn't know the difference. There were days when she ached for David, and then on other days, she

188 ᴄ∾ VANESSA MILLER

ached for Thomas. Her emotions were taking her on a merry-go-round ride, and she wanted to get off.

The phone rang, and Yvonne instantly knew that it was Thomas. There were nights when she wondered why he'd left town in the first place if all he was going to do was send her presents every day and call her every night. "Hello," she said when she picked up the phone.

"Hey! Were you asleep?" Thomas asked.

His voice sounded so richly masculine. "No, I wasn't asleep. I was just studying my Bible."

"Oh, really? What were you studying?" Thomas asked, as if her answer was truly of interest to him.

"A little of this and a little of that." There was no way that Yvonne was going to confess to reading the Song of Solomon, even if it had been only one verse.

"I got a call from our investigator this morning, and he said that he had scheduled a meeting with you for this afternoon. How did it go?"

Yvonne was practically giddy as she said, "Thomas, I'm so glad you recommended that man. He knew exactly how to go in and get the information we needed on Mr. Marvel Williams."

"So, what Clarence said was true? Marvel has been hiring undocumented workers?"

"Apparently, that's how he managed to keep his costs so low and make so much money through the years. But when we get through exposing this man for the fraud he is, he'll probably need an attorney to help him with all the fines and penalties he'll face."

"I told Clarence that I would bail him out of jail on Tuesday if he would agree to tell everything he knows against Marvel at the city council meeting," Thomas said.

"He's not going to do it, Thomas. I've known Clarence Brown for more than twenty years, and that man wouldn't say a mumbling word to me that day I went to see him."

"Trust me, Yvonne, if we let him sit in that jail cell long enough, he'll be ready to snitch and worry about the stitches later."

"Enough about Marvel Williams and Clarence Brown," Yvonne said. "How was your day?"

"Fine—I was out all day visiting pastor friends in Houston, Texas, while Jarrod finished up his last meeting. We have plans to golf with a few friends in the morning, but after that, we'll be back on the road headed home."

"I still can't believe the two of you drove all that way," Yvonne said.

"It wasn't a straight shot. Jarrod and I stopped in five different states. That boy has accounts all across the United States. I'm telling you, Yvonne, he's going to be running the sales department at his company by the time he turns thirty. Mark my word."

"Spoken like a proud papa."

"I am proud of Jarrod." Yvonne could almost hear the smile on Thomas's face over the line. "And I think he feels good about getting to know his old man a little better, also. He didn't fool me when he said he wanted to stop and check in with each of his accounts. That was simply his way of being able to spend more time with me."

Yvonne was so happy for Thomas. She knew that the estrangement between him and his son had been a source of great regret to him, and it sounded like things were finally turning around.

"And the boy is more levelheaded than I gave him credit for where the ladies are concerned," Thomas continued.

"I wish I could say the same thing about my girls where the men are concerned," Yvonne muttered. "I used to think Toya would make the right choice regarding a potential husband, but now that she's dated someone as conniving as Marvel Williams, I simply don't know."

"Toya will be fine. That Marvel guy just took her by surprise. I mean, you have to admit, the guy seemed like a pretty good catch—he's handsome and successful, and who knows what lines he'd been feeding her."

"Well, let's just hope that she doesn't run into another smooth talker anytime soon."

Thomas laughed. "I don't know if we'll be able to save Toya from the smooth talkers. Jarrod hasn't mentioned any other woman but Toya since we've been on this trip. He's been going down memory lane, all the way back to his and Toya's high school days. I don't know, Yvonne. Toya might be the one that got away from Jarrod."

"I sure hope that boy knows how to act this time, because Toya was through with him when he didn't pick her up for senior prom."

"Jarrod still swears up and down that he didn't know Toya expected to go to the prom with him, but I think he just didn't know what he would be losing by taking that other girl—whose name he can't even remember now."

Yvonne shook her head. "To be young and dumb again. I remember how bad I treated David the first time he tried to ask me out. It's a wonder the man ever asked me out again."

Thomas chuckled. "He told me that he liked how feisty you were, and you haven't changed a bit. You've still got that same spirit about you. And now I know firsthand what David was talking about, because it's the reason I fell in love with you, too."

"Thomas!" she admonished him. "Don't say things like that." All week long, they had been having such wonderful conversations. Thomas hadn't declared his love since that day in her office, so she'd let her guard down and had began to relax and go with the flow, enjoying their talks and looking forward to seeing him. But now he was changing the rules. How was she supposed to respond to a man professing his love for her? She'd wondered why Thomas hadn't brought up their relationship, but now that he was, she found herself wishing he wouldn't! She had been truly loved by only one man, and she had spent over thirty years married to him. She knew in her heart that God was not holding her accountable for the promise she'd made to David now that he was dead, but that didn't mean she wasn't holding herself accountable. She'd loved that man for so long and couldn't just stop now and start loving someone else.

"It's the way I feel, Vonnie," Thomas went on. "I know you think that I didn't care for Brenda, and that's why I was gone from home so much. But that's not true. Brenda and I were different, and we had different goals, so things were difficult for us at times, but I loved my wife. The difference between you and me is that I don't feel guilty about allowing myself to feel those emotions again."

Yvonne was silent. She wanted to respond to Thomas, but he was right. She couldn't allow herself to feel such emotions ever again. She had spent thirty years with those emotions, and it just didn't seem right to simply transfer the love she felt for David over to Thomas simply because he was still alive.

"Say something, Vonnie."

"I don't know what to say. This is hard for me, Thomas. Can't you understand that?"

With a long sigh, Thomas said, "I understand." He paused, then changed the subject. "I forgot to ask you if you liked the flowers I sent you yesterday. That bouquet reminded me of you...soft, gentle, and perfect."

"I don't know if that is an accurate description of me, but the flowers were lovely. I brought them home with me."

"Do me a favor, Vonnie," Thomas said with a tone of urgency.

"You know I'll do whatever I can for you. What is it?"

"Go out with me on Monday night."

Now, why'd he have to go and ask something like that? She hadn't been out on a date in so long, she wouldn't even know how to act!

"Just give me a chance, Vonnie. I promise that if you go out with me on Monday night and then you still want nothing to do with me, I'll back off."

"You promise to stop talking about all this love stuff if I still can't see us together after Monday night?" Yvonne asked to clarify.

"You have my word that I'll never again tell you how I feel. But Vonnie, I'll never stop loving you, because what I feel for you is a forever kind of love."

Chapter Twenty-one

*Y*VONNE ASSESSED HER APPEARANCE IN THE FULL-length mirror on her closet door and decided that she liked what she saw. She might be fifty-two, but she could wear an after-five dress better than some women half her age. She had on a yellow silk swing gown with a form-fitting bodice and a beaded sweetheart neckline. The knee-length drape skirt had soft pleats that flowed all the way down to the hem, and her open-toed, beaded gold shoes with two-inch heels were the perfect accessory. It was early September, so she didn't need a jacket, but she grabbed a shawl just in case one of the places Thomas was taking her tonight still had the air-conditioning on.

Thomas had promised to pick her up at six thirty because they had reservations at seven o'clock. Yvonne had been shocked when he'd told her they would be dining at The Whitney because the place was normally closed on Mondays. Thomas must have pulled some serious strings. She wondered which of his vintage cars Thomas would pull up in today. If she could talk that man into purchasing a brand-new car, Yvonne would feel as if she'd accomplished something. Shrugging her shoulders, she said, "Boys and their toys."

Yvonne glanced out the window and was taken aback. Her eyes widened at the sight of the two-tone

Rolls-Royce parked in front of her house. It was dark blue on the bottom and silver on top. She grabbed her handbag, rushed downstairs, and pulled open the front door. That's when she noticed the red rose petals that trailed from her front porch down the stairs, along the walkway, and to the back side door of the Rolls-Royce.

A driver Yvonne didn't recognize stood beside the car and opened the door for her. In his outstretched hand, he held a red rose, which he handed to her. "I was told to give this to the most beautiful woman that I saw today, and to tell her to relax and enjoy herself," he said with a grin.

Taking the rose, Yvonne smiled and thanked the driver. She then climbed into the backseat of the car, feeling like a princess. Thomas was inside, pulling the petals from yet another red rose and tossing them onto the floor.

"What are you doing?" Yvonne asked as she situated herself.

"Making sure that your feet never touch the ground."

He was too good to her. Yvonne simply didn't feel that she deserved all of the time and care Thomas was putting into this evening, and she wanted to make sure that he wouldn't expect too much from her. "Thomas... I don't want you to get the wrong impression."

Thomas held up a hand and said, "If you're going to tell me that you can't see me again, 'Well, then, you should have worn a different dress.'"

Yvonne laughed. She knew exactly where that line had come from. It was her favorite line from the movie *Maid in Manhattan*. Jennifer Lopez's character wore this fabulous dress to a dinner party where she'd planned to break up with a guy, but he took one look at her dress and decided that he wasn't about to let her go.

Yvonne wasn't sure if she looked as good in her dress as Jennifer Lopez had in hers, but Thomas sure made her feel like she did. "Thank you for the compliment, sir."

"No, thank you for wearing that dress. You look beautiful," he said with appreciation in his eyes.

The driver pulled out into the street and drove them to The Whitney. Again, Yvonne thought about all the trouble Thomas was going to. "Why are you doing all this?"

"Hey, I've got one shot at this, so I figured I would pull out all the stops. Just relax and enjoy yourself tonight, lady, because I'm going to win you over."

"I'd say you're trying really hard. What year is this car?"

"Madam, you are riding in the Silver Dawn. It's a nineteen fifty-four Rolls-Royce."

"Will I ever be able to convince you to buy yourself a nice, safe, new car?" Yvonne teased.

"Never. But this one isn't mine. It's on loan to us for the night."

"Well, I thank you for going to the extra trouble. And speaking of that, how on earth did you get The Whitney to agree to serve us on a Monday night?"

Thomas leaned back in his seat and smiled smugly. "Money talks, my dear, money talks."

Yvonne gave him a playful punch in the stomach. "Whatever, Mr. Show-off."

"You ain't seen nothin' yet. Tonight will be just a glimpse of what life with me could be like."

"If this is just a glimpse, I don't know if I can handle the full picture." Goodness gracious, the man was treating her like royalty. Yvonne was well aware that many men in the body of Christ referred to their wives as their queens but didn't always treat them as if they were. She knew quite a few wives who complained that their husbands ignored them, even though they called them "queen" in public.

"Oh, you can handle it, baby," Thomas crooned in his sexy baritone. "I'll hold your hand through it all."

"You don't play fair, Thomas Reed. When David and I were first married, we couldn't buy one Happy Meal at McDonald's. The Lord blessed us through the years, but we still would never have been classified as millionaires. David couldn't just rent out a restaurant or have limousine drivers spread rose petals at my doorstep."

"I'll have you know that I spread those petals across your doorstep myself," Thomas corrected her.

"You know what I mean, Thomas. I have no comparison for what you are doing."

He sat up, took Yvonne's hand in his, and looked deep into her eyes. "Look, Vonnie. I know that what you had with David was special. It wasn't about money, and if I thought you were the type of woman who was looking for a man with money, I certainly wouldn't be wasting my time with you." He paused and took a deep breath before continuing. "And I don't want to be compared to anybody. I want you to judge me by what you see in me. That's all. I can't spend the rest of my life wondering if I'm measuring up to a dead man."

"A dead man who was once a very good friend to you," Yvonne reminded him.

Thomas fell back against the seat and closed his eyes. When he opened them and looked at Yvonne again, he said, "David *was* a very good friend to me. Nothing will ever change that fact. I didn't come back to

Detroit to fall in love with you, Yvonne. I came because David made me promise to help you in any way I could if you needed me. He was fond of reminding me that it was my fault you were preaching in the first place."

Thomas *had* been her hero, even way back before she'd recognized him as such. He'd championed her cause when no one else would stand up for her. She had always been grateful for the friendship they shared. But could she really move their friendship in another direction without bringing a load of guilt on herself?

"Just relax, Vonnie," he said gently. "I won't pressure you. You've got all night to make up your mind."

When they pulled up in front of The Whitney, the driver opened both back passenger doors. Thomas got out and came around to Yvonne's door, where he took her hand and helped her out of the car. Once they were inside the restaurant, a mansion built by lumber baron David Whitney Jr. for his family, the host directed them to the music room. This room was where the Whitneys had entertained their guests with musical performances. Tables filled the room now, but it was still elegant, with authentic Tiffany stained-glass windows and a ceiling mural that featured cherubs dancing on the clouds.

Yvonne pointed up at the angels and said to Thomas, "Did you pick this room because of them?"

"Hey, I need all the help I can get," he said with a shrug. Then, he lifted his head and folded his hands together as if praying to the cherubs on the ceiling. "Please, Mr. Cupid, strike my lady love with your arrow so that I will be the only man in her heart."

Yvonne thought that Thomas's little prayer was cute, but she honestly didn't see his wish coming to pass anytime soon, not with David still taking up so much space in her heart.

They were seated at one of the smaller tables, and they perused the menu in silence while their server filled their water glasses. Yvonne was enraptured by the selections and had a hard time deciding what to order. When the server returned, she finally decided on the risotto with butternut squash, leeks, fennel, and wild mushrooms. Her mouth watered just thinking about it.

Thomas ordered the salmon with spinach, bacon, and Gruyère, and an herbed tomato galette.

"And had you selected a wine to have with your meal?" their server asked them.

"No wine, thanks, but you can bring us some raspberry lemonade or iced tea, please," Thomas replied.

"Certainly, sir."

When their server had left the table, Thomas smiled at Yvonne. "So, are you enjoying yourself so far?"

"I am. You know that I am." Yvonne giggled, then said, "When you take a girl out, you really cover all the bases, don't you?"

"When I've got one shot to win a woman's heart, you'd better believe I'm going to do my best to dazzle."

Yvonne heard soft music begin to play, and she turned to see where the sound was coming from. She dropped her jaw when she saw four men stroll into the room playing violins. It was the most beautiful quartet she had ever heard. She turned back to Thomas and raised her eyebrows. "Oh, you're dazzling me, all right. I'm blown away by how wonderful everything has been."

"The night is young, my sweet Yvonne. I have even more to show you."

"More, Thomas? You're going to be broke by the time this date is over."

Thomas laughed. "I highly doubt that, Yvonne. The good Lord has provided for me both spiritually and financially, so I think we can afford several nights like this."

Thomas was truly a special man. Any woman would be blessed to have him. And Yvonne was beginning to wonder if she could free herself to love again. Thomas clearly had, and he and Brenda had been married for almost as long as she and David. He had grieved over the loss of his wife, but now that two years had gone by, he had given himself permission to love again. And Yvonne was now starting to believe that she would be a fool not to give him a chance. But she couldn't speak her thoughts out loud—not yet, anyway.

"What are you thinking about?" Thomas asked.

The man could read her like a book, but she wasn't about to spill the secrets of her heart. "I just can't wait to taste this food. I know it's going to be delicious, and I haven't eaten a thing since lunch. So, I plan to bash it as soon as it hits the table."

"Well, you'll get your chance in a few seconds, because here comes the food."

Yvonne turned and watched the server as he expertly handled the tray of plates, balancing it above his head as he walked toward them. "They are quick," she said to Thomas.

"We're the only ones in here. They'd better be quick," Thomas said as the server set their plates in front of them.

"It looks delicious," Yvonne remarked. After Thomas had prayed over the food, Yvonne began to devour it. As expected, it was exquisite, and she enjoyed every bite. Even more enjoyable was the conversation she had with Thomas during the meal.

After dinner, the Rolls-Royce whisked them away, and their next stop, as Yvonne soon discovered, was Fox Theatre to see *Dream Girls*. They arrived at ten minutes till nine, and Yvonne assumed that they had tickets for a nine o'clock show. She had momentary apprehension about finding a seat—often, people would sit in the wrong seats because the view was better than where they'd been assigned, and she and David had often needed to find an usher to ask the occupants of their assigned seats to move—but it turned out that her worries were unfounded. She should have known that Thomas would have arranged a private loge for them. Still feeling like a queen, Yvonne practically floated to her seat, ascending the Grand Staircase to the Loge Level.

"Am I passing the test?" Thomas asked with a sly grin on his face.

She wasn't about to give Thomas Reed a bigger head than he already had by telling him how much she was enjoying herself. "Let me see how I like this stage production, and then I'll let you know," she replied with a grin of her own.

"You're a hard woman, Yvonne Milner. But that's all right. I'm up for the challenge."

Yvonne smiled at his comment, but as she looked into his eyes, she realized that she wasn't hard or strong at all. As a matter of fact, her resolve was crumbling. She was weak and needed a way of escape made for her. *Lord, help me*, she prayed silently.

And then, as if the Lord was raining down blessings upon her, the lights turned off in the theatre and the curtains opened. Yvonne turned away from Thomas's mesmerizing eyes, ready to watch the action on the stage.

❧

Thomas was acting cool on the outside, but he was squirming on the inside. As the lights went down in the theatre, he sent up a silent prayer to God, asking Him to make a way out of "No way" and help Yvonne to see that she couldn't live without him. He knew he was praying for a miracle—Yvonne was independent and self-sufficient, and he was up against the simple fact that she could live without him. She didn't need him, or any man, for that matter, and she was more than able to take care of her own business.

Oh, she might have thought she needed him when the board was trying to vote her out of her position as senior pastor, but since that day, Yvonne had been regaining her strength steadily and walking forward into her destiny without David. And, Thomas realized, maybe even without him.

But if God was merciful—and Thomas knew his God to be full of mercy and grace—then He would help Yvonne come to terms with her feelings for him. Thomas knew full well that Yvonne cared for him. He saw it in her eyes every time she looked at him. But trying to get her to admit it to herself, let alone to him, was an entirely different matter. He leaned forward to whisper in Yvonne's ear, but she had her eyes glued to the stage and seemed to be completely engrossed in the production, so he decided not to bother her.

Thomas had only a few more hours to make his case and win Yvonne's heart once and for all, but he couldn't afford to pressure her. No matter how desperately he wanted her to return his love, he just couldn't push her into something that she might end up regretting. If they were going to be together, then she would have to come to him.

Hoping to calm his nerves, Thomas tried to focus on the show and not dwell on whether or not Yvonne would declare her love for him at the end of the evening.

At intermission, he nearly jumped out of his seat. "I'll go get us something to drink," he announced. "Do you want anything to snack on?"

"Are you kidding? I'm still stuffed from dinner. A Sprite will be fine, thanks."

Yvonne beamed up at him, and Thomas almost fell to his knees right there and begged her to be his wife. But he restrained himself and then, as he made his way to the concession area, berated himself for being all kinds of foolish. He kept putting his heart out there, and Yvonne kept slapping it back. Not this time. Thomas was determined to do everything in his power to help Yvonne see just how much he cared for her, but the rest would be up to her. He'd promised her that he would leave her alone if she decided that she didn't want anything more than friendship after their date tonight, and he was a man of his word.

He ordered their drinks and then carried them back to their loge.

"Thank you," Yvonne said as he handed her the Sprite.

He sat down and took a sip of his cola, starting to feel calmer, more confident. Just then, Yvonne reached over and squeezed his knee. "This has been a wonderful evening, Thomas. The most fun I've had in a long time."

Thomas took Yvonne's hand and brought it to his lips, kissing her palm. "You don't know how your words have blessed me, sweet Vonnie."

Before he could release her hand, bright lights began flashing all around them. Thomas turned around to see a man dressed in black snapping pictures of them with a professional photographer's camera.

"What are you doing?" Thomas yelled.

A microphone was pushed in his face by a well-dressed woman with a French manicure, who said, "Thomas Reed, can you confirm that you and Yvonne Milner are having an affair?"

Thomas heard the gasp that escaped Yvonne's mouth and felt ill. "Let's go," he said, pulling her up by her hand.

They exited their loge and marched through the lounge with the cameraman and the woman reporter dogging their heels.

"Why won't you talk to us, Pastor Yvonne?" the woman demanded. "What are you hiding?"

Thomas looked at Yvonne, and the mortified expression on her face broke his heart. He would do anything to shield her from this. He felt somewhat responsible, because he had been so busy worrying about whether Yvonne wanted him or not that he hadn't noticed anyone following him back to their loge. The woman must have seen him pay for two sodas, figured he was with Yvonne, and then followed him.

"Were you involved with Pastor Reed before your husband died?" the woman continued.

With tears in her eyes, Yvonne stopped and turned around to face the woman. "How can you be so cruel? Why would you say something like that?"

Enough was enough. Thomas pulled Yvonne away from the reporters. "You want to know what's really going on?" he yelled.

Yvonne pulled at his sleeve. "Don't do this, Thomas. Don't tell them anything."

"They'll never leave us alone until we tell them, Vonnie. And I don't care who knows how I feel about you."

Thomas turned to the camera and said, "I will admit that I am in love with this woman. But under no circumstances have we ever been romantically involved. We are simply friends. Do I want us to be more?" He paused. "Yes," he finished, then turned and, still holding Yvonne's hand, walked downstairs and outside, where he called his driver to pick them up.

When they got into the car, Yvonne put her head in her lap and cried. Thomas wanted to comfort her, but when he gently touched her shoulder, she pushed him away. So, he sat in silence, waiting for her tears to stop.

When Yvonne finally lifted her head, her beautiful silk dress was blotched with wet spots from her tears and black smudges of mascara. "Why did you tell those people that you're in love with me? Why couldn't you just have left it alone?" she wailed.

"Baby, I'm sorry, but—"

"Don't call me baby," she said through gritted teeth. "I have been only one man's baby, and I don't want to be that for another. Not ever. Do you understand me, Thomas Reed?"

It was coming across loud and clear to him now. Yvonne wasn't upset because they had been accosted by a nosy reporter and a cameraman. No, what had affected her to the point of hysteria was the fact that Thomas had declared his love for her. Well, he'd promised Yvonne that he would leave her alone from now on if, at the end of their date, she still couldn't see them together. And if nothing else had shown him the truth, Yvonne's words just now surely had. Thomas was done playing second to a ghost.

"I'm sorry that my words offended you, Yvonne. I'll take you home, and I won't bother you again."

Chapter Twenty-two

O N TUESDAY MORNING, MARVEL WILLIAMS WENT TO the correctional facility in Flint and set a captive free. Once Clarence Brown's bond was paid, Marvel waited on the man to be released. He was in a foul mood already, what with Toya playing hide-and-seek with him all week, and having something go wrong with Clarence's release wouldn't help.

Marvel wanted the man as far away from Michigan as possible. He wouldn't have put it past Yvonne Milner to pay the man's bail so that he could attend tonight's city council meeting and spill his guts. Marvel would spill the man's guts himself before he allowed him anywhere near that meeting.

"Thanks for getting me out of there," Clarence said when he was released. "I was going a little crazy behind bars."

"Calm down, Clarence. You may be going back there after your trial," Marvel reminded him.

"Still, those were not my kind of people."

The man had just stolen hundreds of thousands of dollars from his church and now had the audacity to claim that he didn't belong among murderers and thieves? Marvel would have laughed in his face, except for the fact that he wanted to convince Clarence that he was on his side. "You sure don't belong with those dregs of society, but that's where Yvonne Milner and Thomas Reed want to make sure you end up."

"Thomas said that he would put in a good word for me at the trial if I agreed to pay back the money and tell them everything I know about your dirty dealings," Clarence said smugly.

"And you believed him?" Marvel laughed out loud as he pulled a thick envelope from his jacket pocket. "I guess you won't be needing this, then." He stuffed the envelope back inside his pocket and started walking away. If Clarence knew what was good for him, he'd take the money and get out of Michigan. But if the man suddenly became afflicted with a do-gooder spirit, then Marvel would follow him and implement plan B.

"W-wait a minute," Clarence stammered. "I didn't say that I was going to help them; I just told you what Thomas said."

Marvel stopped and smiled as he whirled back around to face Clarence. He took two steps toward him, then stopped, pulled out the envelope again, and extended it toward Clarence. "There's a Greyhound bus leaving in less than fifteen minutes. Be on it, and you've got yourself two hundred grand."

"Well, what are we waiting for?" Clarence asked, grasping for the envelope. "Get me to the bus station so I can get out of here!"

Marvel whisked the envelope out of reach. "I'll give this to you after I drive you to the bus station."

"I understand—you don't trust me. Fine. Point the way to your car. I'm ready to go."

When they reached Marvel's BMW, Clarence said, "Hey, why don't you give me the keys, let me drive this baby for old times' sake?"

"You must be crazy. I'm not about to let you drive my car."

"You didn't mind me driving it when you wanted to pretend it was stolen," Clarence pointed out as he opened the front passenger door and got inside.

Marvel slipped into the driver's seat and started the car. "That was then, and this is now," he said as he sped away.

"Oh, I see. I've done your dirty work, and now you just want me out of your face."

Marvel didn't respond.

"That's all right," Clarence said. "Pretty soon, you'll see that I'm not the one you should have been worried about."

"Oh, yeah? Who else should I be worried about?" Marvel asked, gripping the wheel. He was extremely tired of Clarence and just wanted to be done with him.

"How's Toya?" Clarence asked.

The way he asked—as if he knew that things weren't right between him and Toya—really ticked Marvel off. "What's Toya got to do with this?" he demanded.

"Oh, I'm not saying another word until I get my money. Now, if you want to know what's up, I suggest you hand over that envelope." Clarence held out his hand expectantly.

But Marvel didn't budge. He kept driving until they reached the bus station, then pulled his car into the parking lot and braked to a stop. Before Clarence could get out of the car, Marvel turned menacing eyes on him and grabbed his shirt collar. "Whether you know it or not, I spared your life today. Don't tempt me to regret it," he growled. "Now, I asked you a question. What do you know about Toya?"

Clarence wrenched out of Marvel's grip and leaned against the door. "Look, don't get mad at me because you can't keep track of your woman," he said, smoothing his shirt.

"You better start talking."

"All right, all right. Toya came to see me last week. She told me that she read the e-mail I sent to you and that she wanted to know more about the undocumented workers you hired. I didn't tell her anything. But Toya is a lawyer. I'm sure she can find things out on her own if she wants to."

Marvel shook his head. It made sense to him now why Toya had suddenly distanced herself, claiming that she had so many meetings and deadlines that she couldn't spend any time with him. All of that had started the day after he'd allowed her to use his computer. Marvel could have kicked himself. He'd forgotten that his e-mail account had been open, not that he ever would have guessed that Toya would snoop around in there. He'd been trying to figure out a way to destroy Yvonne but still keep his relationship with Toya intact, not wanting to lose her. But that didn't matter to him anymore. It seemed that Toya was just as low-down and conniving as her mother.

Marvel turned on Clarence again. "This is all your fault. If you hadn't kept bothering me about that money, this never would have happened."

"Maybe you should have just paid me in the first place, and then I wouldn't have bothered you at all."

Marvel rolled his eyes. "I wish I could take you back to jail and get a refund. You are really worthless, you know that?"

"Look, just give me my money, and I'll get out of here. Isn't that what you want? For me to be out of here before the city council meeting tonight?"

Marvel took the envelope out of his jacket pocket and handed it to Clarence. "Yeah, get on out of here. I don't care where you go, just don't come back here unless it's with a police escort."

"You're a funny man, Marvel," Clarence said. As he got out of the car, he muttered something else that Marvel couldn't quite make out.

As he sped away, though, it came to him: "But I think Toya's going to have the last laugh on you tonight." He gripped the steering wheel so tightly that his knuckles turned an angry red. He was losing control of the situation. He had risked his entire plan just to have Toya.

Marvel's father had been in the same situation years ago with his wife. The woman had been a total ingrate. All she'd ever done, in Marvel's memory, had been to whine about how many times Carter Williams had hit her. And then, one day, she'd been determined to make the hitting stop—the day she'd finished reading *Girl, Free Yourself.* Yes, Jamica Williams had left her man and tried to start a new life without him, just as Toya was attempting to do. But Carter hadn't let that happen, and neither would his son. Toya would regret the day she decided to turn against Marvel Williams.

He made it back to Detroit in fifty minutes flat and headed straight for the law firm where Toya worked. There was an empty spot two cars down from Toya's. Perfect. It was three in the afternoon; he could stand to wait until she got off work. She would probably leave around five or five thirty if she was planning to rat him out at the city council meeting, which started at seven. Marvel checked his glove compartment for his Glock 17 semi-automatic pistol, which he had a license to carry, thank you very much.

Around four o'clock, Marvel's stomach started to growl. He wished he'd stopped at Subway and grabbed his favorite sub: turkey, ham, and pepper jack cheese on wheat. Thinking about it only made his stomach growl louder. But it would have to wait until he'd taken care of his treacherous girlfriend.

At four thirty, his cell phone rang. It was Toya. She had been playing him for a fool for the past week, so he had no problem playing along. With a huge smile on his face, Marvel pressed "Talk." "Hey, baby! I've been thinking about you all day."

"I've been thinking about you, too. I'm sorry that I've been so busy these past few days. But I was hoping that you'd let me make it up to you this evening."

"Oh? And how do you plan to do that?"

"How about dinner? My treat."

"I'd love to, but I have to be at that city council meeting tonight." If this meeting weren't so important, he would have loved to go to dinner with Toya just to see what she was trying to pull.

"I was thinking about leaving work now. That way, I could pick you up at five. We could eat early, and you'd have plenty of time to get to your meeting."

His workaholic girlfriend was willing to leave work early, *and* she was offering to pick him up? She was really trying hard. He was kind of sorry that he was about to spoil her plans. Just for fun, though, he said, "Yeah, dinner sounds good. Hurry up and get off work. You can pick me up at my house."

"Great! I'll leave in ten minutes."

Marvel smiled with self-satisfaction. He was done with Toya. He had tried to be so good, not wanting anything to spoil their relationship, but all bets were off now. And Miss Toya was going to get what was coming to her.

Ten minutes later, he smiled as he watched his lovely girlfriend—soon-to-be ex-girlfriend, thanks to what Clarence had revealed—rush out of her office building.

He removed his pistol from the glove compartment, stuffed it in his waistband, and stepped out of the car.

Toya slowed her pace when she noticed him standing by the trunk of his car. She frowned but then recovered and gave him a warm smile.

"What are you doing here? And why didn't you tell me you were waiting on me?" She turned her head to the left, then right, as if she were looking for someone.

His smile matched hers. "I wanted to surprise you, baby. We haven't spent much time together, and I was missing my boo."

She gave him a hug and kissed him on the cheek. "So, do you want to leave your car here and ride with me to the restaurant?"

"No, I want you to get in my car," he said, still smiling.

"I don't want to leave my car at the office. Why don't you just follow me?" She looked around the parking lot again.

Marvel wrapped his hand around Toya's arm, gently at first, but as he opened his jacket and showed her his gun, he tightened his grip. "Get in my car now, Toya."

"W-what's the problem, Marvel?"

"Get in the car." He shoved her toward the passenger door.

"All right, all right. You don't have to push."

"And you didn't have to betray me," he said as he opened the door, shoved her inside, and slammed it shut.

He locked the car from the outside, then ran around to the driver's door and unlocked it so that he could get in. Turning the key in the ignition, he said, "I hate to spoil your dinner, but I have other plans for you."

"What's wrong with you, Marvel? Will you at least tell me what's going on?" Her eyes were wild with fear.

"Why didn't you tell me that you read that e-mail from Clarence Brown? If we're in a relationship, then we shouldn't keep secrets, Toya."

"What are you talking about?" she screamed. "Have you lost your mind or something? You'll go to jail for kidnapping me!"

"Who am I kidnapping? You just called and invited me to dinner. Remember?"

"I didn't ask to be shoved into your car at gun-point."

"Hey, this is just the way we get down. You know how we do it, how we joke around and kid with each other. And as soon as I get you to my house, I'm going to kid around with you a little more...after I tie you up." He smiled at her as if he were offering to draw her a bubble bath.

"Why are you doing this, Marvel? I thought we really had something."

"I'm just getting you before you get me. Do you think I really believed that you wanted to have dinner with me?" He looked at her. "What were you going to do, put something in my drink to knock me out so that I wouldn't be able to make it to the city council meeting?"

Toya didn't respond.

"You and your mother thought you were going to rat me out at this meeting tonight, but I'm about to change the good pastor's mind."

"And how are you going to do that?" Toya defiantly asked, as if she weren't riding with a man with a gun in his pants.

"Call her."

"No."

Marvel pulled the gun out of his waistband and pointed it at Toya. "Call your mother."

"What did she ever do to you? Why are you trying to destroy her ministry?"

"It's personal. Now call," he barked.

Toya pulled her cell phone out of her purse, pressed a button, and held the phone with shaking hand to her ear. Several seconds later, she said, "Mama, I'm so sorry. I should have listened to you."

"Hand me that phone," Marvel said. He snatched it away from Toya, who had started crying in a high-pitched, panicked sort of way. "Hey, Pastor Yvonne," he said coolly. "This is Marvel."

"What do you want?" Yvonne shrieked. "What are you doing with my daughter?"

"She's my girlfriend, remember?"

When Yvonne didn't reply to that, Marvel continued. "Anyway, I just wanted you to know that Toya is going to be otherwise occupied until after the city council meeting. I'm the only one who knows where she'll be, so I suggest that you think long and hard before sharing anything about my business dealings at this meeting tonight."

"He's got a gun," Toya screamed.

"Don't you hurt my daughter!" Yvonne yelled.

He held his hand to the back of Toya's head and gently moved it down her neck. "Oh, I could never hurt Toya. But you can...just as you always hurt innocent people. It's up to you, *Pastor Yvonne*." He hoped that she could hear the depth of his contempt. "Is Toya going to get hurt? You decide."

Chapter Twenty-three

I WOULD NEVER HURT MY DAUGHTER, OR ANY OTHER IN-nocent person for that matter," Yvonne managed. How could this be happening? How could she have left her daughter vulnerable to this evil man?

"That's not exactly true, now, is it?" Marvel screamed back at her. "You hurt innocent people all the time. Children grow up motherless and fatherless because of your stupid teachings."

Yvonne realized that she was not talking to a rational person. Something deep inside of Marvel was broken. She didn't want to say anything that would set him off further, so she simply asked, "What do you want me to do?"

"Oh, so now I'm in charge, huh?" he sneered.

"Just tell me what you want, and I'll do it," Yvonne practically begged. "Just don't hurt my daughter."

"Just don't hurt my daughter," Marvel mimicked in a high-pitched voice.

Tears of fear were streaming down Yvonne's face. She had lost a husband. No way was she prepared to lose a daughter. "Whatever you want, you can have it. You want the church to move so you can have the land, then we will move. You don't have to hurt Toya."

"Listen to the sound of a mother's love. You're will-ing to give up everything for Toya, aren't you?"

"I told you I would. You can have the land."

"What if I want you to stop preaching altogether? And not to write any more stupid books?"

Yvonne had a feeling that this thing with Marvel had been about her all along. It had nothing to do with the land the church was on. But why did this young man want her to stop ministering to God's people? "Marvel, I don't know why you are waging a personal vendetta against me when I've done nothing to you."

"Ha!" he sneered. "I knew you wouldn't agree to that. Not even to save your own daughter's life."

Father God, I need You right now, she prayed silently, desperately. *I cannot deny You or Your will, because I know why I was put on earth—to help bring Your children to salvation and then into closer relationships with You. But this man has my child. I know You allowed Your Child to be destroyed for the good of mankind, but I'm not You. I'm not strong enough to bear something like this. So, I'm begging You in the mighty name of Jesus to send help. Send Your angels, Lord.*

"You're praying, aren't you?" Marvel asked sarcastically.

"You'd better believe it." Yvonne spoke with authority now. "And I can promise you this, Mr. Williams: my God will not allow you to hurt Toya."

"If you go to that meeting and discuss my business, you're going to see just how powerless your God is. And don't call the police, or she's dead."

Yvonne heard the click that ended the call. "Wait! Wait!" she screamed. "Don't hang up." But he was gone. She called Toya's phone but didn't get an answer. After trying her daughter's phone three more times, Yvonne decided to call someone else.

There was no answer at Thomas's house, so she tried his cell phone. It rang once and then went straight to his voice mail.

Yvonne needed help fast. She was afraid to call the police because of Marvel's threats. She dialed Elder Conrad. When he answered, she said, "I don't have much time to talk, Elder. I need you to get a message to everyone who signed up for the prayer chain. Tell them that even though today is the last day of the prayer vigil, it's also the day when we need the most prayer. Tell them to pray for Toya's safety, and that I might be able to do what needs to be done at the meeting tonight in order to save our church."

"Is Toya in trouble, Pastor?"

"I'm sorry, I can't tell you anything more. But please, Elder, please, have them pray as never before."

"I'm on it," Elder Conrad said.

Yvonne hung up the phone and fell on her knees. She wanted to call the police, but if Marvel was telling the truth, calling the cops just might get her daughter killed. So, she would call on Jesus instead and pray that He would make a way out of "No way."

All over the city of Detroit, prayer warriors were falling on their knees and praying for God to show up and show out on this day—the day that they needed Him the most. The city had been pushed back and held down by economic woes for a long time, but today, none of that mattered. From Rosa Parks Boulevard, where many houses sat abandoned and vacant, to the Joseph Barry Subdivision, just east of the mayor's mansion, prayers were going up to heaven. In the suburbs of Royal Oak, Berkley, Sterling Heights, and Troy, prayers were going up to God concerning Christ-Life Sanctuary and all of its members.

Detroiters routinely tell visitors not to get off the highway where I-75 and I-94 meet, but today, visitors could have gotten off the interstate using that exit without thinking twice about it, because a dear old woman by the name of Lillian Thornton was lying on her couch, praying. She'd had both knees replaced, so she didn't try to get on her knees anymore, but her prayers were just as powerful when she was lying on her back.

Mother Thornton had been a member of Christ-Life Sanctuary for fifteen years. In recent months, she had stopped attending the church, but it had nothing to do with a faltering faith in Pastor Yvonne. The woman who had transported her back and forth to church for the past ten years had died three months ago, and Mother Thornton had no other way to get to church. When the evangelistic team at Christ-Life had come to check in on her a few weeks ago, they had arranged for a bus to pick her up once a week, and she'd attended every Sunday service since.

Mother Thornton had joined the prayer chain but decided that since she was retired and had the entire day to herself, she wasn't going to pray for her sched-uled hour alone; she was going to pray all day. And she wasn't praying only that Christ-Life Sanctuary would get the victory today, but also that her neighbor-hood would be healed and the hoodlums on the streets would come to know Jesus.

In Highland Park, Beverly Carson was calling out a special prayer for the leadership of Christ-Life and their families, which included Thomas, Yvonne, Tia, and Toya. Debra had no idea just how much they really needed her prayers at that moment. She was just being obedient to the Lord and praying during the time period she had signed up for.

Thomas slammed his fist into the steering wheel. Why had he allowed Toya to talk him into this foolish plan? She had asked to borrow his classic 1964 Mustang convertible, saying that if she picked up Marvel in a car like that, he wouldn't be so suspicious about her offer to drive him to dinner. The plan had been for Thomas to then come to the restaurant and drive away in the Mustang while Marvel and Toya were in the restaurant having dinner. When they went to leave, Toya would pretend that the car had been stolen, just as Marvel had done to her a couple of months back. Marvel would therefore be tardy for the city council meeting, giving Yvonne enough time to reveal everything she knew without Marvel being there with his slick answers.

But when Thomas pulled his Mustang into the parking lot at the law offices of Wilson, Brickholm, and Wiley, he saw Marvel open his jacket and Toya's eyes widen with fear as Marvel grabbed her arm and shoved her into his car. Thomas had kept his cover so that he could follow them whenever they drove away.

Now, Thomas was following a few cars behind Marvel. He was determined not to let the madman out of his sight. Toya was like a daughter to him, and there was no way he would let anything happen to her. But when he picked up his cell phone to call the police, the battery was dead. He hadn't charged the thing in two days. He'd had no reason to. It wasn't as if he had been expecting a call from Yvonne.

Now, he regretted allowing his anger toward Yvonne to affect his emotions to the point that he hadn't bothered charging his phone. What was he going to do? If he stopped at a pay phone, he'd lose Marvel's trail, and there was no telling what he'd do to Toya. "My God, my God, we need Your help!" Thomas shouted in a voice loud enough to carry a prayer straight to the throne of God.

Chapter Twenty-four

"YOU DO REALIZE THAT YOU ARE GOING TO BE AR-
rested, right?" Toya said, apparently trying to
talk some sense into him. "There is no way out of this
but prison."

Driving down the street like a dope man running
from the law, Marvel said, "If I'm in prison but you're
dead, which one of us is better off?"

"Why are you doing this, Marvel? What did I ever
do to you?" Toya was screaming at him. Anger flashed
in her eyes.

But Marvel had just as much anger and attitude.
"You betrayed me, that's what you did. Just like my
mother betrayed my father. And I'm going to give you
just what he gave her."

"I don't have anything to do with what happened
between your mother and father."

"Oh, yes, you do. Your mother is the reason my
mother is dead and my father is still in prison."

"That's ridiculous, Marvel. My mother doesn't even
know your parents!" Toya screamed.

Marvel drove wildly through the streets of Detroit. He'd made so many swerves and U-turns that
he'd almost forgotten where he was trying to go. "Your
mother wrote that stupid book, *Girl, Free Yourself!*"
he screamed back at her as he made another U-turn.
"And my mother read it!"

Toya rolled her eyes. "So what? I don't see the relevance."

"You wouldn't," Marvel sneered. "But my weak-minded mother suddenly found the strength to leave my father after reading that idiotic book by *Pastor Yvonne Milner.*" He spoke Yvonne's name as if it were poison that he needed to spit out of his mouth before it killed him.

"My mother didn't have anything to do with what your mother did."

"She didn't put the gun in my father's hand, either, but he still killed my mother. And I still blame yours."

"That's totally irrational," Toya said.

"It might be irrational to you, but it's all that I've thought about since the day my father was sentenced to prison." He pulled up in front of an abandoned house on Rosa Parks Boulevard and gave Toya a lop-sided grin. "Honey, we're home."

Thomas was having a hard time keeping up with Marvel. The man was swerving all over the place and turning down random streets as if he knew someone was following him. Somehow, Thomas managed not to lose Marvel, in spite of his out-of-control driving. He was not about to let Toya out of his sight.

Just then, Marvel sped up, and Thomas accelerated his speed to stay with him. He only prayed that he wouldn't get stopped by the police. Soon, though, Thomas didn't think he had to worry about that, for Marvel had just turned off the main road into an area where even the police feared to tread.

When Thomas rounded a corner, his worst nightmare came into view. Police cars were barreling down the street with sirens blaring in hot pursuit of a car that was about to crash into him head-on. Thomas couldn't survive a hit like that, especially considering the speed both his car and the other were going. So, he swerved, hoping and praying that the other car would bypass him.

But that didn't happen. The moment Thomas swerved, the other guy lost control, and his car spun round and round, as if it were some demented carnival ride that wouldn't stop. Thomas slammed on his breaks.

The next thing he knew, he was trapped next to the spinning car, and the police had the street blockaded. Several officers got out of their patrol cars, pulled their guns, and waited for the car to stop spinning. Thomas looked over and saw that the car was slowing down but also inching closer and closer to him. He slid over into the passenger seat, opened the door, and jumped out of the car just as the impact from the other car sent his classic 1964 Mustang convertible into a tailspin of its own.

On the ground, holding his knee, which had gotten injured as he'd jumped out of the car, Thomas watched as his Mustang fought with the bigger and bulkier Buick while the cars swung back and forth. By the time the car fight was over, it was clear that his Mustang had lost. So much time and money had been spent restoring that car to its former glory that he was saddened to see it destroyed in such a senseless way. But he didn't have time to dwell on it. He got up from the ground and hobbled down the street.

"Hey, where do you think you're going?" one of the officers yelled. "You need to file a report about your car."

"I can't stay," Thomas yelled back as he continued down the street. "My goddaughter has been kidnapped."

Yvonne got off her knees and stood up. She had been in her prayer position so many times today that her knees were beginning to ache. A soft whisper in her ear said, *The Lord has heard you.* She smiled, believing that everything would be all right.

The meeting started in half an hour. She picked up the file on Marvel and his dirty dealings from the coffee table, then grabbed her purse and keys.

Tia came into the room before she could get out the front door. "You're not leaving without me," she told Yvonne.

Yvonne put her keys in her pocket and turned to face her daughter. Tia's hands were on her hips, and her shoulders were rolling as if she were preparing for a fight. "It's only a city council meeting, Tia. I don't need you there with me tonight. Why don't you stay here and get some rest?"

"I'm going," Tia declared. "When I came home earlier, I could tell that something was wrong. You won't tell me what it is, so I'm going to this meeting to find out for myself."

"Get your hands off your hips and stop talking to me like you're my mother or something."

"I'm not trying to be your mother, but I am worried about you. I tried calling Toya to see if she was going, but I couldn't get a hold of her. So, I'm going."

Giving up all pretense, Yvonne slumped her shoulders and sighed. "Tia, baby, do you want to sit down?"

A terrified look crossed Tia's face as she lowered herself silently to the couch. Yvonne sat down next to her and put an arm around her shoulders. "You're right, honey. Something is going on. But I don't want you in the middle of it because I don't want you or the baby to get hurt. So, please, do what I'm asking and stay home."

"But how can I help you if I'm at home and not with you?"

Yvonne smiled at her daughter. Tia's experiences during this pregnancy had changed her, helped her to grow up. Yvonne liked what she was seeing in her daughter, and at that moment, she knew exactly how Tia could help. "I do need you, Tia. And Toya needs you, too."

"What can I do?" Tia asked eagerly.

"Well, honey, I'm not sure how to say this, so I'll just tell you: Marvel has kidnapped your sister."

"What?" Tia exploded.

"Just listen, hon. I don't have much time. Marvel doesn't want me to reveal the information I have on him at the city council meeting, and that's why he's holding Toya. He claims that he'll let her go after the meeting as long as I keep quiet about him. But I believe that God will provide us the victory in both areas. So, stay here and pray that Toya comes home safe and sound, and that I will be bold enough to do what I must at this meeting."

"Oh, Mama. No!"

"I know, hon. This is a hard one. But we have to be strong. God is a way-maker, and I am standing in faith. Will you stand with me, Tia?"

Tia's eyes had filled with tears. "I want to, but I don't know if God is even interested in any of my prayers."

"Didn't you tell me that you had already asked God to forgive you for the sins you committed?"

"Yes...."

"Then, you have to believe by faith that God has done just what you asked. I need you to believe, Tia. Can you do this for me?"

Tia hugged her. "I'll stand with you, Mama. You go to that meeting. I'm going to get on my knees and pray for you and Toya."

"Thanks, Tia." Yvonne kissed Tia on her forehead, then stood up and gathered her purse.

Before she was out the door, Tia was already on her knees, starting to pray. "Oh Father, You know that I love You. I have made so many mistakes in my life, but I believe that You have forgiven me for them all. And I thank You for Your love, mercy, and grace. Right now, I am coming before You to humbly ask You to please help my mother and sister...."

Chapter Twenty-five

*M*OTHER THORNTON LOOKED UP AS AN OVERWHELM-ing, all-consuming light appeared in her living room. She couldn't make out the image, but she lived her life in expectation of seeing the manifestations of God in action. She sat up and asked, "Is that You, Lord?"

The light diminished, but then she noticed that her front door was wide open. Mother Thornton got off her couch, grabbed her cane, and walked over to the door to close it. That's when she saw the expensive car parked in front of the empty house next door. Her neighbor, Vera Sue Reeding, had lived next door to her for over thirty years. They had watched out for one another before and after their husbands had passed. Vera had gone home to be with the Lord last year, and, ever since, there had been one drug dealer after another trying to use Vera's house to sell poison out of. But Mother Thornton ran each one of them off.

She was a woman who knew no fear, because she knew her God. She stepped outside and slowly walked toward the car. Those knee operations hadn't done her much good, and she often wished that she had just left well enough alone and bought herself a cane like the one she was stuck walking with now, anyway.

She made her way to the car and checked to see if the door was locked. It was locked, but that wasn't going to stop Mother Thornton. She started attacking the car with her cane, looking for the sweet spot that would set the car alarm off. When she found it and the alarm went off, Mother Thornton continued beating on the car.

Thomas had run down two different streets in search of Marvel's car. His knee had gotten pretty banged up from the car accident, but he wasn't feeling the pain. He ran on pure adrenaline and the overwhelming need to find Toya. He couldn't let her down, not on something as big as this. When he reached the end of the street, there was still no sign of Marvel's car. At this point, he was tempted to go back to the accident scene and ask one of the officers to help him find Toya. He turned around and started running back up the street when he heard the sound of a car alarm.

In this neighborhood, Thomas figured that car alarms probably went off all the time, but for some reason, he couldn't ignore this one. He turned in the direction of the noise and started running toward it.

"Lady, what is your problem?" Marvel yelled as he walked out of the abandoned house and found an old lady beating on his BMW.

"I want you to get away from 'round here," the woman yelled back. "No drug dealing is allowed on this here street."

As the woman kept up her racket, the front doors of several houses opened, and various neighbors came outside to see what all the commotion was about.

Marvel took a quick look around and decided he had better go. He grabbed his keys out of his pocket. "Look, lady. I don't have time for this. I have someplace to be, anyway." He unlocked the car door, jumped inside, and sped off.

When Yvonne arrived at the Coleman A. Young Municipal Center, she was surprised to see many familiar faces—members of Christ-Life who had come out for the city council meeting. They were lined up outside and holding up signs with encouraging messages, such as, "Praying for you!"

Tears welled in Yvonne's eyes as she read those signs. The church members probably would never know just how much she really needed their prayers right now. Or maybe God had sent an angel to whisper her needs into their ears.

Yvonne walked inside the municipal center and followed the signs to the room where the meeting was being held. It had started already, as she was fifteen minutes late, and when she walked in, she noticed that the governor was in attendance, seated right next to the mayor.

She found a seat in the second row and tried to be patient as she listened to the other issues being discussed. While she waited for her issue to come up, she made sure to pray for Toya. Without some divine help, she couldn't go through with exposing Marvel Williams for the monster he was while worrying about her daughter's safety.

Yvonne wanted to believe that God would make a way of escape for Toya, but would she truly be able to put her daughter's life in jeopardy, not knowing whether or not she was safe yet? There had to be another way. And Yvonne was counting on God to show it to her.

Thomas rounded the corner onto Rosa Parks Boulevard just in time to see Marvel jump in his car and speed off. "No!" he yelled.

On the sidewalk ahead, an older woman turned to face him. He recognized her immediately as Mother Lillian Thornton, a longtime member of Christ-Life. Never had a familiar face been such a welcome sight.

"Pastor? Pastor Thomas?" she said, slowly making her way in his direction. "What's wrong?"

"H-he's got...my goddaughter...Toya...Yvonne's daughter," Thomas stammered, panting as he tried to catch his breath.

"Who?" Mother Thornton asked.

"Marvel—the man who just drove off."

"That man was alone. He left by himself."

Thomas clasped his hands behind his head and began turning in circles, starting to panic. "Oh God, where is she?" he shouted. "Where is she, God?"

"He came out of that abandoned house," Mother Thornton said calmly as she pointed to a dilapidated-looking structure. "Maybe Toya's in there."

Thomas bolted for the house. His knee almost gave out as he bounded up the porch steps, but he endured the pain. He threw open the screen door, rushed into the dark house, and searched one room after the next, praying that he would find Toya alive. He would never be able to look Yvonne in the eye again if he brought her daughter home in a body bag.

"Toya! Toya!" he yelled as he passed through what appeared to be the living room, kitchen, and first-floor bedroom.

He was at the bottom of the stairs, getting ready to search the second level, when he heard muffled sounds coming from behind a closed door in the hallway. He rushed to the door and yanked it open. There sat Toya, tied to a filthy toilet. Duct tape bound her mouth, and her eyes spoke the terror she could not voice. The entire room smelled of mold, and as he stepped forward to start untying Toya, two mice scurried past him out into the hallway.

The terror in Toya's eyes turned to relief as Thomas untied her. Thankfully, the rope had not been fastened in a way that was difficult to undo.

When she was free, she jumped up and pulled the tape off her mouth with a terrible ripping sound. "We've got to get to the council meeting!" she blurted out. "Marvel is going to kill my mama."

"Not as long as I'm living, he won't." And Thomas meant every word.

Yvonne was still praying for Toya when she heard the door open and saw Marvel walk in. She watched as he took the empty seat directly in front of her as if it belonged to him. It was all she could do not to jump up and announce to everyone in the room that he had kidnapped her daughter. She saw the governor lean over and whisper something to the mayor. When the mayor finished speaking with the governor, he called an end to the current discussion and opened the floor for discussion on the eminent domain seizure of property for a new business district.

Yvonne prayed for strength.

"Pastor Milner," the mayor addressed her, "it has come to my attention that you have information concerning the new factory we intend to build in the community in which your church resides."

Tapping the folder that she held against her thigh, Yvonne looked up and into the eyes of Marvel, the monster, who had turned around in his chair. His eyes were filled with a hatred and violence that unnerved her. At that moment, she feared that he had already harmed Toya, but she took a deep breath and decided to trust God. He had brought her this far, and she was sure that He would finish what He had started. She saw the hand of God, and it was working in her favor.

The prayers of the saints had brought the governor to this meeting of City Council, and Yvonne knew that the mayor, who had been too busy to meet with her and Thomas a few months ago, was addressing her now only because of whatever information the governor had just shared with him. Thomas also had a lot to do with this. How she wished he were here with her now. But she understood why he wasn't. She'd pushed him away, and he wanted nothing more to do with her or her problems. God was with her, though. She could feel His presence, and it gave her strength.

Taking a deep breath, Yvonne stood up and summoned her voice. "Mr. Mayor, Mr. Governor, members of the council: I certainly do have information that I believe bears on your decision to build the factory. The information is regarding certain unethical business dealings of Mr. E. Marvel Williams."

"Excuse me, Mr. Mayor," Marvel said as he stood up, "but do you normally allow the citizens of this city to slander upstanding local businessmen at these meetings? I am simply trying to move this city forward by putting unemployed people back to work."

"We need those jobs!" a man shouted from the back of the room. "Let the man build his factory!"

Yvonne turned around and saw a little old lady stand up to shout back, "Then let him take *your* home and build his factory in *your* neighborhood!"

A buzz erupted through the room as everyone started speaking at once. While that was going on, Marvel turned around again and gave Yvonne another menacing glare. "I'm the only one who knows where Toya is," he said quietly so that she alone could hear. "Do you really want to do this?"

Yvonne felt a holy boldness rise up in her that far outweighed any confidence she'd felt since learning that Marvel had kidnapped Toya, and she knew for sure that the saints were still praying. "My God knows where Toya is, and He will bring her to me," she said firmly.

Marvel laughed.

Yvonne didn't pay attention to him. She moved into the aisle and marched up to the front, then turned around and faced the room. "This man," she said, pointing at Marvel, "does not plan to help the unemployed of Detroit." Everyone quieted down as she continued. "He cannot help the unemployed of Detroit because he hires undocumented workers." She turned around and placed the file folder in front of the mayor. "I have evidence that proves Mr. E. Marvel Williams has arranged for illegals to be smuggled into this country and has forced them to work for less than the minimum wage. And if you check into his factory in Flint, Michigan, you'll find even more evidence to support my claim."

"American jobs should go to American workers!" yelled a male voice from the middle of the room.

His comment set off an eruption of shouts and a flurry of movement. The people were fighting mad and shouted about how they had suffered too long with high unemployment to let some factory owner come into their town and give away their jobs to people who shouldn't even be in this country.

The mayor pounded his gavel several times, trying to quiet the crowd. "Sit back down," he shouted. When no one did, he repeated, "Sit back down, or the guards will put you out of here."

Slowly, the crowd began to sit down, but low murmurs could still be heard all across the room.

The mayor looked down at Marvel. "Can you explain this?"

"Why should I have to explain any of this nonsense? Pastor Yvonne must have ulterior motives for spreading all these lies about me. Her church was about to go into foreclosure—until her boyfriend paid off their debt. If anything, I'd say that Pastor Yvonne is the one who needs to explain to her congregation just what's going on with her and Pastor Thomas Reed." Marvel turned to face the crowd. "I'm sure you all remember seeing those pictures of pastors Yvonne and Thomas in a steamy embrace."

Yvonne refused to respond to Marvel's sensationalized version of her relationship with Thomas. Instead, she told the council, "If our church was behind on its mortgage payments, it was largely because Mr. Williams paid one of our board members, also the finance director, to embezzle money from Christ-Life."

"I did no such thing," Marvel objected. "Are we going to continue listening to these lies by a disgraced preacher, or are we going to rule on whether or not I can have that land so I can bring some jobs to this town?"

The governor spoke next. "How many employees do you have in your Flint location, Mr. Williams? How many of them are paying taxes, and how many are undocumented?"

As Marvel opened his mouth to respond, the door opened once more, and Thomas came in, followed by Toya. Yvonne felt as if her heart would explode with joy, even though Thomas looked as if he'd been tied to a pole and beaten all day long, and Toya was almost as haggard-looking as he. "Thank You, Lord Jesus!" she exclaimed.

Forgetting all about the proceedings, Yvonne ran to Toya and wrapped her in a tight embrace. "I'm so glad you're all right," she said through her tears.

"Thanks to my hero, here," Toya said, smiling at Thomas.

Yvonne turned to Thomas and gave him a hug. "Thank you, Thomas. Thank you so much...for everything."

They broke apart when Toya screamed, "Stop him!"

Yvonne looked up and saw Marvel running to a side door.

"What's going on?" the mayor demanded.

"That man kidnapped me!" Toya exclaimed. "You can't let him get away. He needs to be arrested!"

Chapter **Twenty-six**

$\mathcal{M}$ ARVEL HAD GOTTEN AWAY, THE SECURITY GUARDS reported when they returned, breathless, from chasing him down to the parking lot. But Yvonne wasn't worried. She knew that justice would finally catch up with that scoundrel.

Joined now by Thomas and Toya, she stood before City Council once more. "We are here because we firmly believe that our church and neighborhood should not be bulldozed to make way for a business that does not have the best interests of the citizens of Detroit in mind."

The room erupted once more, this time with cheers and shouts that echoed the sentiment that Yvonne was right—Marvel and his factory needed to go back where they'd come from.

At the mayor's command, they gradually quieted. When the room was silent, he spoke. "In light of the information you have provided, Pastor Milner, I think it's safe to say that we will launch a thorough investigation into the other plant Mr. Williams owns in Michigan. If the allegations are found to be true, he will not be permitted to continue doing business in Michigan, let alone build a new factory here. I guarantee you that."

Cheers went up all around the room, and Yvonne, Toya, and Thomas came together for a group hug. Soon, the meeting was dismissed, and the three of them hung around to speak with various residents and officials to find out what they should do if a similar issue ever came up again.

As they were leaving, Thomas said, "I guess we're going to need rides."

"You two caught a cab?" Yvonne asked him.

"No, cabs don't usually service the neighborhood we were in. One of Mother Thornton's neighbors gave us a ride."

"Thomas, I would really like it if you could tell me what happened. You look like you were on the losing end of a fight."

His shirtsleeves were ripped and his pants torn; he had bruises on his arms and face. Yet he merely shrugged. "Hey, my sixty-four Mustang is in worse shape than I am," he joked.

Yvonne gasped. "Not the car you bought while you were on the road with Jarrod?"

"The one and only. They delivered it yesterday. But I'll tell you more about that later."

When they reached Yvonne's car, she handed Thomas the keys. "Here. I know it isn't a classic, but you can drive my car."

"These new cars take all the fun out of driving," he said with a grin, then got into the car.

"But at least you know it's not going to die from old age while you're driving down the street," Yvonne remarked as she slid into the front passenger seat and Toya got in back.

"Hey, only one of my cars ever died on me while I was driving it, but sixty-three was a bad year for cars in general."

Yvonne and Toya laughed, and Thomas joined in.

He pulled out of the parking lot but didn't turn in the direction Yvonne had expected him to. "I think we'd better go to the police station and file a report against Marvel before we do anything else," he said, apparently knowing she would question him.

"Why didn't you and Toya go straight to the police after you found her?" Yvonne asked.

"We had to make sure you were okay first, Mama," Toya spoke up from the backseat. "Marvel had me terrified. He blames you for his mother's death, and I honestly thought he was going to try to kill you."

"Oh, my. What a troubled man! Why on earth would he blame me for his mother's death? I've never even met the woman!"

"Evidently, she left his father after reading your first book, and then his father killed her."

"That's horrible!" Yvonne gasped.

"You'd think he'd blame his father," Thomas said.

"Exactly!" Toya exclaimed. "I thought Tia had bad taste in men, but I'm the one who fell for the psychopathic, government-defrauding businessman who was planning to kill my mother."

"Okay, you win," Yvonne said with a giggle. Thomas laughed along with her.

"I don't know what you two find so funny. This is serious. I dated a man who wanted to ruin my entire family. I didn't even believe poor Robbie when he told me that Marvel had put something in his drink. I was so taken in by Marvel that I even accused you of being paranoid."

And that did hurt, Yvonne admitted to herself. She and Toya had always maintained such a close relationship, she'd never imagined that her daughter would believe some guy over her own mother. But it had happened, and they would have to get past it. "We all make mistakes, Toya," Yvonne said, turning around to face her daughter. "I don't think you should beat yourself up too bad. Marvel is a very engaging young man, and you aren't the only one he fooled. He worked his charms on the government of Detroit, as well."

"Well, this won't happen again," Toya assured her. "From now on, instead of looking at how fine or business-savvy a guy is, I'm going to be checking out his love life."

Now Yvonne was scared. "His *what*?"

"His love life," Toya repeated. "I want to know if he is in love with God before I even wonder about whether I could fall in love with him."

"Amen to that," Thomas said as he pulled up outside the police station.

Yvonne and Thomas went inside with Toya and sat quietly as she filed charges against Marvel. She was an attorney, after all, and would know exactly what to tell the officers.

When Toya was finished filing her complaint, Thomas asked her if she wanted to be driven home or if she'd prefer to spend the night at Yvonne's.

Toya turned to Yvonne and smiled sheepishly. "At the risk of sounding like a big baby, I think I'd rather stay at your house tonight. Is that okay?"

Yvonne nudged her shoulder. "It's more than okay. Tia is at the house, so the three of us can have a slumber party!" She put an arm around Toya's shoulders as the three of them walked back to the car.

"It makes me feel better knowing that the three of you will be together tonight," Thomas said as they got back in the car. "Hopefully, the police will put Marvel behind bars before he can try anything else."

"Are we going to get you home next?" Yvonne asked him.

"No, if it's okay with you, I'll take you home and then bring your car back in the morning. I want to make sure that you and Toya get home safely."

"Thanks, Thomas. We appreciate everything that you've done for us," Yvonne said as she gazed at the profile of the man who had put his life on the line to save her daughter today. Thomas had been there for her time and time again, even when she had mistreated him and pushed him away. She wished with everything in her that she could give him what he wanted, but she still was not sure she could do that. So, she was relatively quiet for the rest of the ride, careful not to say anything that might give him the wrong impression.

In the course of her quiet contemplations, however, Yvonne wondered about the thoughts that had been filling her mind in the past several days. The formerly vivid image of David was getting dimmer and dimmer, and even now, Thomas seemed to be taking up more and more space in her heart and mind.

Logically, Yvonne understood that David was gone—he had been for almost two years now, and he had been seriously ill a full year before his death. It was natural that she would think about him less and less as the years went by. But could she get comfortable with the idea that another man might be able to fill the space in her head and heart that David alone had occupied for so long?

Thomas's hand touched Yvonne's and squeezed it in a gesture of reassurance. "Get that worried look off your face. The police will catch Marvel. If they don't, I will. I promise you that."

"I hope you're right." Yvonne played along, knowing that Thomas probably thought she'd been thinking about Marvel and his dirty deeds all this time.

"Hey! Where is your faith, woman?"

She smiled at Thomas's effort to lighten the mood. "My faith is intact," she assured him. "The saints have been praying for us all day. And even though my daughter was basically kidnapped, I felt at peace most of the day, firmly believing that God would see us through this."

"So, maybe you should deliver a sermon about peace in the midst of storms this Sunday," Thomas said.

"I just might do that."

They continued their light banter for the remainder of the drive, and Yvonne felt more and more at peace. But when Thomas pulled up in front of her house, her peaceful world was rocked once more. An ambulance and several police cars were parked in the driveway, and the front door was wide open, with medics and police going in and out of her house. She jumped out of the car and ran up the walkway, Thomas and Toya close on her heels. "What's going on?" she demanded of no one in particular. "What are you doing in my house?"

"Mama, Mama!"

Yvonne rushed in the direction of Tia's voice. "Baby?"

"I'm so glad you're here! I tried to call you and Toya but couldn't reach either of you."

In the living room, they found Tia, lying on a stretcher. Two medics began wheeling her out of the room. "What's happened, honey?" Yvonne asked, walking alongside them. "Marvel didn't show up here, did he?"

Tia shook her head. "I started bleeding. I don't know what's wrong. I'm only six months along, so I shouldn't be bleeding. Right, Mama?"

"No, baby, you shouldn't be bleeding," Yvonne said as she followed the stretcher outside. Fear was all over Tia's face, and Yvonne wanted to say something to calm her, but with everything that had happened that day, she couldn't readily come up with something.

That's when Thomas spoke up. "Brenda spotted when she carried Jarrod. We worried about it, but he turned out just fine. You will be all right, baby girl, so don't sweat it."

Tia smiled through her tears. "Thanks, Uncle Thomas. You always know the right thing to say."

As the medics lifted her into the ambulance, Toya hollered up to her, "We're coming, Tia. We'll be right behind you, and we'll see you at the hospital."

"Okay," Tia hollered back. "I'll see you when you get there."

After making sure that everyone was out of the house, Yvonne locked the front door, then got back in the car with Toya and Thomas, who drove them to the hospital. The emergency room parking lot was full, so they had to park in the lot across the street.

They got out of the car and were crossing the street when a pair of headlights suddenly lit the road. A dark sedan was coming so fast that it could have been drag racing. And it was headed directly at them.

Yvonne froze in the middle of the street. Toya screamed. Thomas pushed them both out of the way, but he couldn't clear the car's path in time. The impact was so great that his body spiraled in the air before falling back to the ground.

To Yvonne, everything seemed to happen in slow motion. When she saw the car hit Thomas, all she could do was chant, "Jesus, Jesus, Jesus."

Toya was still screaming, but Yvonne shook her and said, "Go into the hospital and get help." Then she dropped into a crouching position and crawled over to where Thomas's body lay. She felt as if she were crawling in slow motion, too—like somebody had changed her settings, and she could move no faster than the speed of slow. Blood was on the ground. Thomas had a gash on his head, and he wasn't moving. "Wake up!" she yelled at him. "Wake up this instant, Thomas Reed! Don't you die on me."

Yvonne wanted to shake him, but she was afraid that any movement might cause him more harm. She leaned down and put her head against his chest, not caring that they were in the middle of the street and that the person who had just hit Thomas could come back for her. She just wanted to be near him. Tears rolled down her cheeks as she pleaded, "Please be all right, Thomas. Please, just be all right. Lord Jesus, help him. Let him live."

Chapter Twenty-seven

*Y*VONNE WENT BACK AND FORTH BETWEEN TWO HOSPI-
tal rooms for a few hours. When Robbie arrived
and promised to stay with Tia in her room, Yvonne
went to the hospital chapel. She really wanted a stop
button that she could press to end this horrible ride
and get off.

When they'd left the city council meeting, she had
felt such a sense of peace. It had seemed that things
were finally going their way. The church would not be
bulldozed so that Marvel could build a factory and hire
all the undocumented workers he could find, and Toya
was safe and sound, even though she'd been shaken
up a lot today. Yvonne had been so thankful.

Then, she'd gone home and found an ambulance
waiting to take Tia to the hospital, and now she was
at the hospital in this quiet little chapel, sitting on a
wooden bench and praying not only for Tia, but for
Thomas, as well. She was grateful that Tia had at least
stopped bleeding. The doctor on call thought that she
would be fine, but he wanted to keep her overnight for
observation.

Thomas, however, was a different story. Yvonne's
heart ached as she recalled the sight of him being
struck by that car and then flying in the air like a
paper-thin kite. But when he'd come back down, his

body had hit the ground with such a thud that Yvonne had known he'd need multiple casts for his broken bones—if he survived. Closing her eyes in an attempt to shut out reality, Yvonne prayed harder than she had in a long while. "Don't let him die, God. I told him that I didn't need him. But the truth of the matter is, I do."

She opened her eyes and looked down at the wedding and engagement rings she still wore, even though her husband was no longer living. Tears welled up in her eyes as she put her hand around the precious jewels that had sparkled on her left hand for over thirty years but suddenly seemed not to belong there anymore. She twisted the rings off her finger and held them in her hands. It was time to say good-bye to David because love for another man now resided in her heart.

Lying down and stretching herself out across the pew, she cried tears of sorrow and joy. It had taken her a while to move forward from the place where her heart had once been. When she sat up again, she wiped the tears from her face and said, "I have to let you go, David. My heart belongs to Thomas now."

She opened her purse, placed her rings in an inside compartment, stood up, and left the chapel. In the waiting room, she found Toya sitting with Jarrod, who must have just arrived. His head was down, yet he was fidgety, shaking his leg and tapping his fingers on his forehead. Yvonne went over to him, sat down beside him, and gave him a hug. "It's going to be all right, Jarrod. We've got to believe that," she said, trying to convince herself to believe, as well.

"I can't lose him now, Auntie Yvonne. I feel like he and I just became friends. I don't want to say good-bye to him yet."

She didn't want to say good-bye, either. She knew firsthand how hard good-byes could be. Turning to Toya, she asked, "Did the doctors say anything while I was at the chapel?"

"Nothing new, Mama. He still hasn't woken up... that can't be good." Toya's face was already wet from crying, but as she said those words, fresh tears rained down her face.

At that moment, another surge of holy boldness rose up in Yvonne. She stood up and said with all confidence, "I'm not going to let anybody's thoughts or doubts destroy Thomas's chances of survival. The two of you are staying in this waiting room. I'm going back to his room to wake him up. That man is going to live. You'll see."

She turned and walked away without looking back. As far as she was concerned, Toya and Jarrod had better pull themselves together, because nobody they knew was dying in this hospital tonight.

In Thomas's room, it felt chilly, so Yvonne rushed over to him and pulled the covers up over his hospital gown. Then, she stood next to his bed and gazed down at him. Even with the bandage on his forehead, the man was just irresistible. How she had managed to deny him all these months was beyond her understanding. If she could go back in time and do things differently, she would have cherished her husband more while he'd been alive, and then she wouldn't have felt obligated to put him on a pedestal after he'd died.

Yvonne had finally realized that her hesitation about loving Thomas had more to do with regret for all the opportunities she'd missed when it came to loving David. She had been too busy chasing after success in her ministry to be content with success in her marriage. She'd always thought that there would be plenty of time for loving later. But when David had gotten sick, Yvonne had been filled with so much guilt and regret that she'd made a promise she could no longer keep.

She put her hand on Thomas's chest. "I need you to listen to me," she said softly. "I have decided to love you, Thomas Reed. But I'm not promising my love to another dead man. So, if you want the love I have to offer, I suggest you wake up so you can receive it."

Her words weren't all warm and fuzzy; she knew that. But she didn't have time to compose something eloquent. She had to let Thomas know that she was waiting for him if he would just decide to live. "Can you do that for me, Thomas? Can you wake up so that I can love you?"

Tears streamed down Yvonne's face as she said the words she had held back for the past few months. She was in love with Thomas Reed. It wasn't the same as the love she'd had for David. No, this love was different; it was new, and she was happy. She cracked a smile as she realized just how wonderful it felt to finally admit her love for this man. She leaned closer and whispered in his ear, "I love you, I love you, I love you."

The monitors started going off with loud beeps, and nurses began rushing into the room. They asked Yvonne to step out for a moment. She stood in the hall, biting her nails and praying that this was not the end for them.

Several minutes later, the nurses walked out of the room as if everything was all right with the world. Yvonne wanted to scream at them and ask how they could be so calm when the man she loved was struggling to stay alive.

One of the nurses took off her latex gloves and walked over to Yvonne. "He's okay. Something must have excited him. He's probably just dreaming." With that, the nurse turned and walked away.

Yvonne tiptoed back into Thomas's room but didn't go near the bed. Instead, she sat down in a chair and tried not to bother him. She knew full well that it hadn't been a dream that had excited Thomas but her declaration of love whispered in his ear. A nurse brought Yvonne a pillow and a blanket, and she thanked her before propping her feet on another chair and closing her eyes.

The next thing Yvonne knew, someone was shaking her. "Huh? Huh? What's wrong?" she asked, feeling completely disoriented.

"It's me, Auntie Yvonne. I want to sit in here with my dad. I promise to be positive," Jarrod said.

Yvonne sat up, and Jarrod sat down in the chair her feet had been propped on.

"What time is it?" she asked him.

"A little after eight."

She rubbed her eyes, trying to focus. "Where's Toya?"

"I took her home so she could change clothes. She's at work now."

"Thanks for taking her home," Yvonne said as she stood up. "I need to go check on Tia. You keep your dad company, and I'll be back."

Yvonne went upstairs and stopped in the doorway of Tia's room. Robbie was lying on a cot at the foot of Tia's bed and snoring. Tia looked wide awake, propped on an elbow and channel surfing. "So, how is my baby girl doing this morning?" Yvonne asked when she walked into the room.

"Much better, Mama," Tia said, beaming at her. "How's Uncle Thomas? I feel so awful that he got hit by that car because he was coming to the hospital to see me."

"It's not your fault, sweetie, and I don't want you to blame yourself. The person driving that car is responsible for what happened to Thomas last night."

"I know, but—"

"I don't want you worrying, Tia. Worrying is probably what got you rushed to the hospital in the first place. So, just concentrate on staying well for my grandchild. Okay?"

Robbie turned over, and his snoring became louder. Yvonne pointed at him. "Do you hear what you'll have to put up with if you marry this man?"

"Leave him alone, Mama. Robbie had a rough night, too. He was so worried about us, I don't think he went to sleep until about five this morning." Tia leaned over and whispered. "He's got a job here in Detroit. He starts next week."

Yvonne smiled. "That's great news, Tia. You get some rest, and I'll come back up to see you before you leave." She bent down and kissed her daughter on the forehead. "I love you."

"I love you, too, Mama."

Yvonne called Toya to make sure she was all right and then headed back to the intensive care unit. When she entered Thomas's room, she saw a police officer standing next to Jarrod at Thomas's bedside with a pen and pad in hand, talking to Jarrod. Yvonne thought it was odd for the officer to be standing there like that when Thomas could not provide any information right now. But then, she heard a voice that brought tears to her eyes.

"It was Marvel Williams," Thomas said. "I looked directly at him as he ran me down."

Jarrod turned around, and Yvonne met his gaze with a questioning look.

"He woke up a few minutes after you left the room," Jarrod said, coming closer to talk to her. "He got a little excited when he noticed that you weren't in the room, but when I told him that you went to check on Tia, he calmed down."

When the police officer left the room, Yvonne walked over to Thomas. "Hey, you," she said.

Thomas beamed up at her. "Is that all you have to say to me?"

She raised her eyebrows in question but then figured he wanted to know how Tia was doing. "Tia is doing fine," she said. "They kept her overnight for observation, and she'll be going home in a few hours."

"That's great, but that wasn't what I wanted to hear." When Yvonne gave Thomas another puzzled look, he said, "I want you to whisper in my ear again."

Laughing, Yvonne said, "You scoundrel. You were probably awake the whole time, just pretending to be knocked out so you could get me to confess my secrets."

"Come here," Thomas said, gesturing with his arm.

She didn't need a second invitation. She sat down on the bed, leaned over, and kissed Thomas as if the doctors had asked her to revive him by mouth-to-mouth resuscitation. When she sat up again, she said, "I love you, Thomas. You will always have my heart."

"I couldn't ask for more than that," he said, wrapping his bandaged arms around her for another kiss.

Epilogue

THREE MONTHS LATER, THEY WERE ALL AT THE HOSPI-
tal again. But this time, it was for a joyous occasion. Tia had just given birth to a baby girl, Jayden
Trinity Carter. She was seven pounds and two ounces
of pure beauty, even if she was still all wrinkly and
reddish-brown.

Robbie sat on the edge of Tia's bed and held his
little girl as if she were some rare, irreplaceable jewel
that could break if mishandled. "She's so beautiful. I
can't believe this is really our daughter," Robbie said
with tears glistening in his eyes.

"Hey, speak for yourself," Tia said. "I am more than
capable of making a beautiful child."

The room erupted in laughter. Thomas was standing next to Yvonne with his hands on her shoulders.
They had weathered many storms in the short time
they'd been together, but with the help of the Lord,
she and Thomas had come through it all. The au-
thorities still hadn't located Clarence Brown or any
part of the four hundred thousand dollars he'd stolen
from the church, but they were thankful that Marvel
had been arrested and would soon be serving time for
his deeds.

Yvonne was also thankful that over the past few
months, Thomas had been patient with her as she'd
grown more comfortable with accepting her love for him.

Toya sat in the rocking chair next to the window, waiting for a chance to hold her niece. Behind her stood Jarrod, who smiled as he asked, "So, if Auntie Yvonne is my godmother, does that make Jayden my god-niece, or what?"

"She could be just your niece if you'd pick up the pace and ask Toya out already," Tia chided him.

Seeing the embarrassed look on Jarrod's face, Yvonne retored, "Hey, you leave Jarrod alone."

Robbie stood up and handed the baby to Toya, then turned back to Tia and cleared his throat. "Tia? I…uh, I'd like to be more to you than just your baby's dad-dy. I understand why you didn't marry me before, but I've changed. I've been on my job now for about three months and haven't missed a day or gotten written up or anything. I want to be a family. So, what I'm asking is, will you please marry me?"

It's about time! Yvonne thought as she looked at her baby daughter, anticipating her reply.

Tia smiled, but then hesitated. "That depends. Will you come to the wedding drunk again?"

"You know I haven't had a thing to drink in months. I'm a Christian, Tia, and that means something to me. The Lord is helping me to stay sober."

"Well, all right then, Robbie Carter. I guess I'll marry you," Tia said.

The room erupted in cheers. Yvonne had secretly been rooting for Robbie ever since that night at the hospital when Robbie had refused to leave Tia's side. She'd seen then that the boy had grown into a man—a man well able to take care of his family.

"Okay, why don't we give them some privacy?" Thomas suggested.

Out in the hallway, Thomas invited Toya and Jar-rod to lunch with him and Yvonne, but they both declined. She figured that they would probably hang out by themselves.

After they'd said good-bye to the new parents and baby Jayden, Thomas helped Yvonne into her coat, and they headed to the car. Thomas opened the passenger door for her, but before she could get in, he took her hands in his and grinned. "Well, what about you, Yvonne? Do you think you'll ever marry me?"

"That depends," she said with a hint of mischief in her voice. "Are you going to come to the wedding drunk?"

"Drunk in the Spirit and drunk in love? You bet," Thomas answered, then wrapped his arms around her and kissed her tenderly.

When he released her, Yvonne gave him a sly smile. "Well, in that case, I guess I have no choice but to marry you."

"You always have a choice."

Yvonne shook her head. "I never had a choice, Thomas. You stole my heart, and I don't ever want it back."

"So, it's mine forever?"

Yvonne closed her eyes. She had promised David forever love, just as he had to her, and now she realized it was impossible to promise something she had no control over. When she opened her eyes and found the man she loved gazing at her, she said, "How about for 'as long as we both shall live'?"

About the Author

*V*ANESSA MILLER OF DAYTON, OHIO, IS A BEST-SELLing author, playwright, and motivational speaker. Her stage productions include *Get You Some Business*, *Don't Turn Your Back on God*, and *Can't You Hear Them Crying*. Vanessa is currently in the process of writing stage productions from her novels in the Rain series.

Vanessa has been writing since she was a young child. When she wasn't writing poetry, short stories, stage plays, and novels, reading great books consumed her free time. However, it wasn't until she committed her life to the Lord in 1994 that she realized all gifts and anointing come from God. She then set out to write redemption stories that glorified God.

Second Chance at Love is Vanessa's first series to be published by Whitaker House. Book one in the series, *Yesterday's Promise*, was number one on the Black Christian Book Club national bestsellers list in April 2010, and it was followed by *A Love for Tomorrow*. *A Promise of Forever Love* completes the series.

In addition, Vanessa has published two other series, Forsaken and Rain, as well as a stand-alone title, *Long Time Coming*. Her books have received positive reviews, won Best Christian Fiction Awards, and topped best-sellers lists, including *Essence*. Vanessa is the recipient of numerous awards, including the Best

Christian Fiction Mahogany Award 2003 and the Red Rose Award for Excellence in Christian Fiction 2004, and she was nominated for the NAACP Image Award (Christian Fiction) 2004.

Vanessa is a dedicated Christian and devoted mother. She graduated from Capital University in Columbus, Ohio, with a degree in organizational communication. In 2007, Vanessa was ordained by her church as an exhorter. Vanessa believes this was the right position for her because God has called her to exhort readers and to help them rediscover their places with the Lord.